CUMBRIA LIBRARIES

D1099957

Also by Shane Hegarty

The BOOT series

BOOT

BOOT: The Rusty Rescue

BOOT: The Creaky Creatures

SHANE HEGARTY

The Shop of IMPOSSIBLE ICE CREAMS

Illustrated by
Jeff Crowther

HODDER

HODDER CHILDREN'S BOOKS

First published in Great Britain in 2022 by Hodder & Stoughton

1 3 5 7 9 10 8 6 4 2

Text copyright © Shane Hegarty, 2022
Illustrations copyright © Jeff Crowther, 2022

The moral rights of the author and illustrator have been asserted.

All characters and events in this publication, other than those clearly
in the public domain, are fictitious and any resemblance to
real persons, living or dead, is purely coincidental.

All rights reserved.
No part of this publication may be reproduced, stored in
a retrieval system, or transmitted, in any form or by any means, without
the prior permission in writing of the publisher, nor be otherwise circulated
in any form of binding or cover other than that in which it is published
and without a similar condition including this condition being
imposed on the subsequent purchaser.

A CIP catalogue record for this book
is available from the British Library.

ISBN 978 1 444 96249 9

Typeset in Adobe Garamond Pro by
Palimpsest Book Production Ltd, Falkirk, Stirlingshire

Printed and bound in Great Britain by
Clays Ltd, Elcograf S.p.A

The paper and board used in this book
are made from wood from responsible sources.

Hodder Children's Books
An imprint of
Hachette Children's Group
Part of Hodder and Stoughton
Carmelite House
50 Victoria Embankment
London EC4Y 0DZ

An Hachette UK Company
www.hachette.co.uk

www.hachettechildrens.co.uk

For Tim and Marie,
my mum and dad

Chapter 1

The first thing to know about Limpet is that his favourite ice cream was vanilla.

There was nothing dangerous about vanilla ice cream. Nothing that might jump out and attack you.

Whatever might attack you from an ice cream? you ask.

Limpet knew *every* way an ice cream might attack you. He had written them all down in his notebook of Things That Might Go (Badly) Wrong.

A chocolate flake might go up your nose and poke your brain.

Strawberry sauce might cause a wasp to get stuck on your lip. And then another

wasp might attack you to rescue its wasp
friend.

Sprinkles might make you sneeze really loudly
and Limpet's one wobbly tooth might fall out in
the sneeze and rocket up someone's nose and
that person would have to live with a tooth up
their nose for the rest of their life and . . .

. . . No, vanilla would do just fine for Limpet.
Nothing could go wrong with vanilla.

Unless it was vanilla in a cone. Cones always got soggy bottoms and dripped on the ground and Limpet could slip and fall.

He did like other ice creams. His mum loved making them, and he enjoyed helping her. Together they had made raspberry ripple, tutti frutti, rocky road, and tuna and celery.

OK, he didn't like tuna and celery ice cream too much.

The second thing to know about Limpet is that he did not like being called Limpet one bit. That was a nickname his mum gave him as a baby. He wouldn't tell anyone why.

He liked his real name, Liam. He even liked his middle name, Patrick. And he didn't mind his surname, Lewis.

Liam Patrick Lewis was a proper name for a ten-year-old. Limpet was not.

The third thing you need to know is that everyone called him Limpet anyway.

And that's it. That's all you need to know about Limpet for now.

Nothing else at all.

Chapter 2

"Ta-dah!" said Limpet's mu—

Chapter 3

—Oh wait, there's a fourth thing you should know about Limpet.

With his mum and evil little sister, he had just moved to the seaside town of Splottpool.

Today would be the strangest day of his life. And things would only get stranger after that.

But it didn't start strange.

It started with those happy words . . .

Chapter 4

"Ta-dah!" said Limpet's mum.

She pointed at the tiny ice cream shop on the quiet promenade by Splottpool's foamy grey sea.

"Ta-dah?" asked Limpet. He was confused because the ice cream shop was closed.

"Ta-*duh*," said Limpet's little sister, Eve, poking her head out from under Mum's armpit and screwing up her face to let him know he was stupid.

Everyone loved Eve because they believed her to be a cute, puppy-eyed, lively six-year-old.

Limpet knew different. He knew she was six years of pure evil.

"Ta-*don't* argue," said Mum to both of them. "This ice cream shop will be the start of our new lives in this lovely little seaside town."

All Limpet saw in the lovely seaside town was a stony beach, a long promenade, closed shops and an empty crisp packet blowing in the breeze.

The crisp packet stuck to Limpet's face. He peeled it off, worried the packet was full of diseases or cheese and onion crumbs or – worst of all – cheese and onion flavoured diseases.

He would add that to his notebook of Things That Might Go (Badly) Wrong later.

"Are we buying ice cream?" he asked, while scrubbing his tongue.

"Oh, we're buying ice cream all right," said Mum, excited. "We're buying *lots* of ice creams. Special ice creams. *Impossible* ice creams."

Impossible ice creams? wondered Limpet.

"This isn't just any ice cream shop," said Mum. "This is *our* ice cream shop. We bought it. We open in exactly one week. Next Saturday! How exciting is that?"

"Wow," said Limpet.

"Woo-bleurffhh!" said Eve, while sticking her tongue out at Limpet.

"We're going to make ice creams no one has ever tasted before," said Mum.

She hugged Limpet tight around the shoulders, and he squirmed because he was ten and hugging your mum in public wasn't something ten-year-olds did. Even though he secretly liked it.

"Where's the key to the shop?" he asked, wriggling away from his mum's squeeze.

"With this man," she said.

Limpet almost leaped out of his trainers at the man standing *right behind* him. A man with *enormous* eyebrows. Like a family of spiders lived on his face.

It wasn't just his eyebrows. His whole head was hairy. He had bushes in his ears, weeds up his nose, and his beard grew in every direction.

Up, down, sideways, backwards, in circles.

His head looked like a nest, but on top sat a small, pink, paper hat. It was one of those ice cream parlour hats that looked like an upside-down boat.

"MARSHMALLOW EXPLOSION!" the hairy man barked at Limpet.

"W-w-what?" murmured Limpet, really worried some of the man's eyebrow hairs would blow off in the wind and land in his mouth.

"That was MY FAVOURITE ice cream," said the hairy man, staring at Limpet like he was trying to make lasers come out of his eyes. "What do YE like?"

"Limpet likes boring ice cream," said Eve.

"Stop it, Eve," warned Limpet.

"I like ice creams that make your head pop off," said Eve.

The hairy man lifted his hat and underneath it, buried in his wiry hair, was a big key like the kind used to open castles. "I made ice creams here since I was a BOY."

Turning the key in the shop's lock, he pulled hard on the stuck door. "Mint LEGENDS. Chocolate WATERFALLS. Blueberry—"

"SEAGULLS!" shouted Limpet's mum as the door opened and a big white bird flapped out from behind the dusty counter with an ice cream cone in its mouth. A second seagull waddled out the door with its head covered in blue sprinkles.

The shop was not much bigger than a large shed, with a counter at the front and a kitchen in the back. The seagulls had knocked over jars and forced open cupboards. It was a mess.

"Yummy – cola bottles," said Eve, peeling a sticky sweet from the counter and popping it in her mouth.

{SPECIALS}

The man glared at Limpet through his wild eyebrows. "Aye, folks used to queue DOWN THE STREET to get my ice creams. Do ye know why I stopped?"

Scared of all that hair, Limpet kept his mouth firmly shut as he shook his head.

"Because of *THAT* . . ." The hairy ice cream man pointed beyond the buildings across from the promenade, towards a giant shopping centre that loomed over the streets and blocked out the morning sun.

"There's a big ice cream shop there. *Mr Fluffy's Mega Emporium of Amazing and Spectacular Ice Creams.* It's like an ICE CREAM SUPERSTORE."

The idea of an ice cream superstore made Limpet drool. He wiped his mouth with his sleeve.

"Mr Fluffy wanted nothing more than to CRUSH my little ice cream shop." The hairy man crushed his pink paper hat with his hairy knuckles. "And he DID."

Limpet's heart sank.

Mum picked up a jar of liquorice sweets that had been tipped over. A snail crawled out of the jar. "We'll be making very different ice creams to Mr Floppy or Fluffy or whatever his name is," she said, peeling off the snail and putting it on the windowsill so it could escape . . . slowly. "We'll make ice creams you'll not get anywhere else on the planet."

Limpet's heart rose.

"Mushroom and cheese ice cream . . ." Mum said.

Limpet's heart sank again.

"Carrot and garlic ice cream," she continued. "And I have a recipe for the greatest spaghetti ice cream you've ever tasted."

Limpet's heart now felt like it was in his foot. *Spaghetti ice cream! With tomato sauce and pasta*

*and that stinky sprinkly cheese? How could that
even work?*

"People want new tastes these days," Mum
said. "Surprise tastes."

The man's eyebrows rustled as he raised them
high. "Well, it's YOUR shop now, so YE can
make SPIDER ICE CREAM if you want," he
said.

"Please don't make spider ice cream, Mum,"
said Limpet, because that's the kind of thing she
might *actually d*o.

"Now, if ye don't mind, I'll be off," said the
man. "I have a new passion in life.
SKATEBOARDING!" He turned and flicked up
a skateboard Limpet hadn't even noticed was
there.

Standing on the skateboard with his eyebrows
blowing in the wind, the man said, "Good luck
to ye and your WEIRD ICE CREAMS." He
skated away, almost running over a seagull that

was pecking at some chocolate flakes on the floor.

His words swirling in the breeze, the hairy man shouted a warning before he disappeared. "DON'T GET CRUSHED BY MR FLUFFY!"

Chapter 5

Opening an unbroken jar of marshmallows,
Limpet's mum checked to make sure the pillowy
sweets weren't mouldy before offering one to
Limpet. He shook his head. He didn't want to
bite into a marshmallow and find a worm inside.

Eve took three marshmallows,
shoved them in her
mouth, chewed them
noisily, and then
yawned to show
Limpet the sticky
mush stretching
like pink cobwebs
across her teeth.

So evil.

"Everything is going to be A-OK," Mum said, half talking to herself.

Mum said this a lot. She had said this especially often during their move to Splottpool.

Limpet really wanted everything to be A-OK too. So he decided he should smile and be as sunny as a blue sky. Even if the sky was grey right now in Splottpool.

But he didn't think mushroom and onion ice cream, or conkers and socks ice cream, or whatever, was going to make *anything* OK.

Vanilla ice cream. That's what would make everything A-OK. Good old-fashioned, not-at-all-weird-or-dangerous vanilla ice cream.

He didn't tell his mum that right now. He wanted to make her happy. And make himself happy too.

"It *will* be A-OK, Mum," he said.

"Me and Eve are going to do a bit of tidying up here, Limpet," said Mum. "You go and explore. You might find new friends."

Limpet took a deep, quiet breath. He took an extra gulp to try and swallow all his nerves and *what ifs* about everything that could go wrong.

Maybe he would make no friends in Splottpool. Maybe he would get hit in the face by a seagull having a sugar rush.

He wanted to stay and help his mum instead, but Eve was looking at him with two marshmallows shoved up her nose.

Pure evil.

Limpet stepped out of the front of the shop.

Thankfully, he wasn't hit in the face by a seagull having a sugar rush.

He was hit on the side of the head by a chicken instead.

Chapter 6

The chicken flapped its wings wildly.

Limpet flapped his arms even more wildly.

He checked his head to make sure it was still there. Yep. His ears were in the right place. His nose was where a nose should be. His wobbly tooth was still wobbling in his gums.

The chicken settled on the path in front of him.

Limpet had not seen many chickens, but on the list of Scrawniest, Patchiest, Baldest, Daftest-Looking Chickens Limpet Had Ever Seen, this one went right to the top.

"What?" Limpet asked the skinny chicken. "Who?"

"*Buk,*" said the chicken.

"Come back, Curtis!" a boy shouted as he ran up the promenade swinging an empty dog lead.

Curtis the chicken dodged one way, then the other, but the boy guessed its every move and pounced, grabbing the chicken.

Tucking the bird under one arm, the boy put the lead around its neck so it couldn't slip free. Then he stood, red-faced and out of breath, while the chicken pecked at his shoes.

"Thanks for stopping Curtis with your face . . ." gasped the boy, who was a little shorter than Limpet. "Curtis doesn't like going for her daily walk . . . The last time she escaped I had to use a fishing net to catch her . . . and a catapult . . . You've a chicken feather in your ear . . . My name's Norman."

Limpet pulled the small feather from his ear.

"Before you say it, I know Norman's an old-fashioned name," said Norman. "I've got five brothers and one sister . . . My dad says I'm called Norman because my parents had so many kids they ran out of names by the time they got to me. What's your name?"

Before answering, Limpet checked his wobbly tooth wasn't going to fly out and up Norman's nose.

"He's called Limpet," said Eve, appearing from the shop with a sugary jelly snake hanging from the corner of her mouth. She sucked it through her lips with a *schloooop*.

"Why Limpet?" asked Norman.

This was top of Limpet's list of Worst Questions in the World.

"Don't even think about saying it, Eve," warned Limpet, because Eve was *definitely* thinking about saying it.

"*Buk-bawk*," said Curtis, briefly flapping off the ground.

"My name's not Limpet, it's Liam," said Limpet. "That's just something stupid my evil sister calls me."

His mother popped her head out of the shop's tiny window. "Limpet!" she shouted out. "It's great to see you've made a friend already." Limpet's face was hot with embarrassment.

"Hello Limpet's mum," waved Norman, accidentally pulling on Curtis's lead. The bird clucked unhappily. Limpet's mum waved back.

"This is our new ice cream shop," said Eve while spraying little bits of sugary snake everywhere. "We're making *impossible* ice creams."

"Don't mind my sister," said Limpet. "She's evil."

"Am not!" protested Eve.

"That's *exactly* what an evil person would say," said Limpet. He walked away quickly, with Norman and Curtis following. Limpet was very pleased he'd said something so funny and clever to Eve in front of this new friend.

"You've a feather in your hair, stupid bird-head!" Eve shouted after him.

Limpet pretended he didn't hear her, but plucked the feather out of his hair when he thought she couldn't see him any more.

Chapter 7

As they walked, Limpet and Norman talked about a lot of things.

They talked about how Limpet had moved from the city, where he still had lots of friends. Like, *millions* of them.

They talked about Curtis and how one of Norman's brothers had found her as a chick, wandering on the side of the road. No one knew where she had come from but when they looked into Curtis's freaky little chicken eyes they couldn't bear to get rid of her.

"*Buk*," said Curtis. "*Buk-bawk*."

Norman said he didn't have an evil sister but he did have an evil older brother who did very evil things like snort at Norman.

Limpet agreed that snorting was a sure sign
of evil.

They talked about Limpet being ten years old,
which Norman thought was really cool because
he was still only nine and two-thirds.

Norman asked why Limpet was called Limpet,
but Limpet didn't want to tell him because it
was embarrassing and a secret. Instead he told
Norman that he knew a boy who knew a girl
whose cousin once drank cola and mints at the
same time and his head *exploded*.

Norman showed Limpet some of Splottpool's
most important sights. There was a long pier
sticking out into the sea. It was closed. Norman
said it was dangerous because a bus full of
tourists once fell through a large hole in it and
their bus was carried over the sea to Brazil or
somewhere.

There was the really tall Splottpool Tower that
people used to be able to go up in until a lift

got stuck. Norman said
that people were in the
lift when it got stuck and
they were never rescued
and their skeletons are
still up there to this day.

Norman also told
Limpet about that really
big shopping centre, with
Mr Fluffy's Mega
Emporium of Amazing
and Spectacular Ice
Creams. Even from far
away he could see it lit
up with pink and yellow
flashing lights and a line
of pink and yellow flags
fluttering over the door.

Limpet thought that
he could smell the

faintest scent of Amazing and Spectacular ice creams, coming from the shop that the hairy man said might CRUSH Limpet's mum's little place.

Thankfully, as they rounded the corner to the town's busy main road, something distracted Limpet from these worries.

A lemon. Just rolling down the street like it was going for a walk. It bumped up against his toe.

"*Buk?*" said Curtis, cocking her head to examine the fruit with her freaky chicken eyes.

Limpet picked up the lemon and felt something strange. Not scary strange. Just *strange*. Like a little bit of energy ran from the fruit to his fingers.

He saw no fruit and vegetable shops nearby. "I wonder where this came from," Limpet said.

"Probably from that roundabout," said Norman, pointing.

The roundabout wasn't really a roundabout, because cars didn't drive all the way around it. It was more like a small, perfectly round island in the middle of the road, with traffic having to swerve to avoid hitting it.

It was covered with lush plants and tall stalks and wide leaves and chunky flowers. There was a rickety shed just visible at its centre. It looked like a tiny garden – an allotment – just like Limpet's granddad had in the city. But he had never seen a garden on a roundabout in the middle of a busy road.

"It's a fairy fort," said Norman.

"A *whatty* fort?" asked Limpet.

"A fairy fort," said Norman. "You can never build over a fairy fort. Bad things happen if you do. I heard a man tried to bulldoze that fairy fort so they could build the road over it. Do you know what happened to him?"

"What?" asked Limpet.

"His head fell off," said Norman.

"His *head* fell off?" said Limpet.

"Yes," said Norman. "Or maybe it was his hat. Yes, that's it. His hat fell off. But it was a *brand new* hat. Anyway, there's a woman who minds that roundabout. She grows fruits and vegetables and things. People say they're *magic*."

"What kind of magic?"

"Strange magic," said Norman. "Like, I've heard the lemons are lucky for anyone who eats them."

Limpet looked at the lemon. It didn't look magic. But it did *feel* sort of magic.

"I don't know if it's true because I don't eat lemons," said Norman. "They make my face shrivel up."

Limpet put the lemon in his pocket and they walked on, back towards the promenade and his mum's ice cream shop.

"Will your shop have 99s and choc ices and all that stuff?" asked Norman.

"Maybe," said Limpet. "My mum likes to make different ice creams with, you know, carrots and whatever."

"Super," said Norman, even though Limpet knew it wasn't super at all.

Curtis the chicken pulled on the lead as she tried to run towards a seagull with its head in a bin. Norman kept a firm hold of the lead. "Do you think your mum will do a seagull ice cream?"

"Urgh, I hope not," said Limpet. "I imagine seagulls probably taste really fishy."

"Oh yeah, me too," laughed Norman.

That laugh made Limpet feel warm and happy inside. It made his worries fade away. His

day was going pretty well now. He had made a
friend. No teeth were up anybody's nose.
Everything was going A-OK.

Then he heard music. Tinkly music, drifting
across the rooftops and through the streets. Ice
cream van music.

Except this was not ordinary ice cream van
music. It was a slow song. A bit out of tune.
Almost a song of doom.

A van came around the corner. A big,
rectangular van with dark windows and bouncy
pink and yellow writing on its side:

MR FLUFFY

Chapter 8

Mr Fluffy's van didn't look so special. It didn't look like it came from the most incredible, dream-crushing ice cream shop ever.

It just looked like a big van with pink and yellow writing on it. There wasn't even a pretend ice cream cone on its roof like most ice cream vans.

Limpet was not impressed.

Mr Fluffy's van stopped close to Mum's new shop, its engines growling.

"I was worried about Mr Fluffy, but that's kind of a boring van . . ." said Limpet.

"Oh," said Norman, looking awkwardly at the ground. "Um . . ."

"*Buk*," said Curtis the chicken.

The driver's dark window rolled down to reveal a tall, thin man with a shock of red hair covered with a hairnet. He wore big sunglasses with mirror lenses.

Limpet's mum appeared at her window to check out the noise. Without taking his eyes off her little shop, Mr Fluffy reached up and flicked a switch over his head. The van burst into activity.

"MR FLUFFY'S MEGA EMPORIUM OF AMAZING AND SPECTACULAR ICE CREAMS" suddenly appeared on the side of the van as a smiling curve of flashing, rainbow-coloured lights.

The tinkly music sped up until it was really catchy disco music. A large metal ice cream cone popped up on the roof. A disco ball rose up from the top of cone, where the ice cream should be. Spinning, the ball reflected sunlit disco sparkles all around the street.

Limpet's jaw dropped. Norman tapped his feet to the disco music. Curtis the chicken tapped her claws.

Limpet looked at his mother over at the shop window. She seemed calm, but Limpet's mouth was still open wide, until a small fly nearly flew in.

"Mr Fluffy's not fluffy at all," said Norman. "We call him Mr *Huffy*. He is the grumpiest, meanest, scariest, grumpiest – did I already say grumpiest? Anyway, he's all those things."

Mr Fluffy rolled up the dark window, disappearing behind it.

"He must make yucky ice cream," said Limpet, hopeful.

"Oh, it's *amazing* ice cream!" said Norman. "And spectacular!"

Kids appeared from every direction, sprinting towards the disco van as if it was life-saving ice cream and only the first one there would get it.

"It's the greatest ice cream you'll ever have. Anywhere. On any planet. In the whole universe," said Norman, before thinking twice. "Except for yours. Yeah, yours will be better. But he has a *secret* recipe. No one knows how he makes ice cream so tasty and scrummy and . . . let's have one now. My treat."

Before Limpet could say anything, Norman handed Limpet the lead. "Be careful with Curtis. The strawberry smell of the ice cream is like the strawberry air freshener I use to stop her chicken coop smelling of chicken poo. She might think the van is her home and try to get in."

Limpet held tight as Curtis tried to pull towards the van with surprising strength for a scrawny, bony bird.

Just before all the kids reached the ice cream van, a squawk blared from the speakers and a stern voice rang out. "There are rules!" the unseen Mr Fluffy announced.

The kids stopped in their tracks.

"No screaming. No grubby hands. No dancing in the queue. No gymnastics. No nose picking. No hair twirling or thumb sucking. And most of all . . ." The shutter on the side of the van sprang open suddenly to reveal tall, thin Mr Fluffy at the counter, his hairnet flashing with hundreds of multi-coloured lights. He glared directly at Limpet.

". . . Absolutely, completely, one hundred per cent *no chickens*."

Mr Fluffy stopped staring at Limpet, slapped his hands on the counter and announced quietly but firmly to the first child in the queue, "Order."

Holding in their giddiness as best they could, even if some couldn't help jig a little as they waited, the kids stepped forward one-by-one to get their ice creams.

Limpet's nose began to tingle with the

sweetest, freshest, fruitiest, ice-creamiest smell anyone could ever imagine. On any planet. In the whole universe.

He saw the colours of the ice cream pouring from the machine on to the cones and being taken away carefully by the kids. The reddest of raspberry ripples. The creamiest of vanillas. Sprinkles that sparkled like sunlight on water.

Every ice cream spiralled perfectly on the cones, curling into long, narrow wisps at the top. A rich chocolate flake stuck out from each one.

"*Buk-bawk,*" said Curtis, and Limpet realised he had drooled on the chicken's head just looking at the ice creams. Even the dangerous, not-vanilla ice creams.

Joining the back of the queue, Norman gave Limpet a small wave. Limpet waved back and Curtis pulled hard on the lead. Enticed by the aroma, Limpet couldn't help but wander closer to Mr Fluffy's big disco ice cream van. Curtis stretched the lead ahead of him.

"No chickens," said Mr Fluffy, not even looking up while handing a sparkling blue ice cream to a little curly-haired girl. Watching the ice cream to make sure it didn't slide off, she stood aside quickly before licking it with a big slurp.

In the line, Norman took one step closer to the counter.

Limpet saw his mum calling Eve back into the shop. They both disappeared inside. Limpet wandered out of sight towards the back of the van.

"*Buk,*" said Curtis.

The van's doors were closed, but red liquid was dripping from a gap at the bottom. It looked like sauce. Thick, velvety, ruby-red sauce. But it smelled different to ice cream sauce. A smell he couldn't quite figure out.

Limpet would tell Mr Fluffy about the leak. Surely that would mean Mr Fluffy would leave their ice cream shop alone and definitely not CRUSH it. He popped his head round the corner of the van.

"Excuse me—" Limpet started, but he was interrupted by a scream from across the street. It came from his mum's shop.

Chapter 9

With a giddy squeal, Eve almost fell out of the shop as she sprinted towards the ice cream van.

"No screaming!" said Mr Fluffy, seeing Eve running towards the orderly queue.

"And no chickens!" he said, spotting Limpet and Curtis at the corner of his van.

Curtis tried to escape her lead, thrashing her wings right into the line of kids waiting for their ice cream. They screamed in fright and delight.

Eve arrived, pushing through the kids only to trip on the chicken's lead and yank it from Limpet's grasp. Free at last, Curtis rose in a feathery mess and flew straight over the van's counter, smacking Mr Fluffy's flashing hairnet and knocking a jar of sprinkles off the counter, before disappearing inside in a tangle of wings and chocolate flakes and sweets and hairnet lights.

The jar of sprinkles exploded in a sparkly cloud on the pavement. A noseful of sprinkles went straight up Limpet's nostrils. He sneezed. His wobbly tooth shot out of his mouth like a bullet, burying itself in the little curly-haired girl's ice cream – just as she licked it.

The girl froze with her blue-stained tongue stuck out. On the end of her tongue was Limpet's tooth.

The girl screamed. Every kid screamed.

They screamed and groaned and laughed and *eeewww*ed.

Limpet moaned "sorrrrrry" from the very deepest part of his tummy where all his worries were stored. Because he really was sorry.

The curly-haired girl scraped at her tongue to get rid of the tooth.

In the van, Curtis the chicken was knocking over boxes of jellies and jars of mini-marshmallows. She flipped the taps so that ice cream poured freely, flooding the floor with raspberry ripple disaster and honeycomb catastrophe.

Eventually, Mr Fluffy managed to fight through the chicken tornado of wings and feathers and sauce and sprinkles to open the van's back door and release Curtis.

One-by-one, he shut down the flowing ice cream machines. Then he took a long, ominous look at the terrible mess in his van, where ice cream sloshed across the floor and multi-coloured chaos dripped from every shelf.

With anger all over his face and a feather stuck to the corner of his mouth, Mr Fluffy turned off the last flashing light on his torn

hairnet and pointed a chocolate flake at Limpet.
It was like a magic wand ready to weave a
terrible spell.

"I. Said. No. Chickens."

Chapter 10

"I didn't mean . . ." said Limpet.

"I said no screaming," said Mr Fluffy, jabbing the chocolate flake at Limpet.

"That wasn't me . . ." he said looking at Eve, who shrugged her shoulders like it wasn't *her* fault.

"I didn't say 'No sneezing teeth into blue ice creams' because I did not think anyone would ever sneeze a tooth into a blue ice cream."

The kids watched on, quiet except for the sound of slurping on ice creams. There was a lot of slurping.

Maybe, maybe, maybe this won't end too badly, thought Limpet.

Mr Fluffy looked up and a fresh egg rolled

off a shelf above him and broke on his forehead.

"Curtis, you did an egg!" said Norman, very proud of the bird held under his arm.

Nope. It was going to end very *badly*, thought Limpet.

"I saw a leak," said Limpet, his voice high with desperation.

"Now there is raspberry ripple in the peppermint," said Mr Fluffy. "There is chocolate in the bubblegum. And there are chicken feathers in *everything*."

"The leak came from the back of your van," said Limpet, eager to make things right.

"And *nobody* wants chicken-feather ice cream," said Mr Fluffy.

"I think it was leaking sauce, but it smelled different," said Limpet.

"No talking," said the so-very-irritated Mr Fluffy, waving the chocolate flake at him.

"It smelled of . . ." started Limpet.

"No more words or I swear by the soul of my father, Mr Horatio Fluffy the Third, you will regret it."

The word had already formed on Limpet's lips. He couldn't help but let it out. ". . . paint," he said.

Mr Fluffy slowly pulled the hairnet from his head and used it to mop sludgy ice cream from the counter.

All Limpet could hear was his own heart *bub-bumb-bub-bumb*ing. Nothing could make this moment worse.

"Our mum is opening the ice cream shop," said Eve.

No. *That* could make things worse.

"She's going to make the *best* ice creams ever. *Impossible* ice creams," said Eve.

Yep. Much worse.

Mr Fluffy casually bit the top of the chocolate flake, grabbed the window handle and shut it with a splash of spilled ice cream. He reappeared at the steering wheel, rolling down the window again.

Holding his microphone, Mr Fluffy stared at Limpet through small, dark eyes that were somehow even scarier because one of them had egg yolk dripping down its eyebrow. "I will *crush* your ice cream shop," said Mr Fluffy, his voice squawking through the van's speakers.

"*Ooooh*," said all the children.

"*Buk*," said Curtis.

"*Ugghhh*," groaned Limpet, wishing his luck would change. He felt the lemon in his pocket, and a little shot of magic warmth went through his fingers.

Mr Fluffy pressed the button above his head. The music slowed. The lights stopped flashing. The disco ball went into the ice cream cone, and the cone disappeared back into the roof. Mr Fluffy drove away.

Limpet felt dizzy. He had worried about Things That Might Go (Badly) Wrong, but even worse and *far* more chickeny things had happened instead.

They could hear the tinny music of doom from Mr Fluffy's van carried on the breeze until it too was gone and all was quiet on the street except for the last of the ice creams being slurped.

Eve suddenly realised something. "What about my ice cream?!"

Chapter 11

The next day was Sunday. Limpet's mum had got the shop cleaned up, and now, with the rows of ingredients arranged neatly on the shop's kitchen counter, it was time to make ice cream.

"We open the shop on Saturday. Just six days away," said Mum. "Just six days to make the best, most impossible ice cream around."

Six days to avoid getting CRUSHED by Mr Fluffy, thought Limpet.

"And I know just what great ingredients to start with . . ." said Mum.

She slapped a big punnet of mushrooms on the counter. Eve took a mushroom and smushed it in her hands.

"What if no one wants mushroom ice cream?" asked Limpet, trying not to hurt his mum's feelings.

"You're right," she said, and grinned mischievously. "That's why I'm going to add *tuna* to the mushrooms." She emptied a shopping bag of tuna tins on to the counter. Limpet caught one before it rolled off the edge.

EXTRA FISHY TUNA CHUNKS
NOW WITH FEWER BONES!

"*Mushroom* and *TUNA* ice cream?!" he gasped.

"Not just *any* mushroom and tuna ice cream," said Mum. "*Homemade* mushroom and tuna ice cream."

"Mum—" complained Limpet.

"We'll make so many incredible new flavours. Onion and tea ice cream. Roast parsnip and gravy ice cream. Chicken and cheese. Prawns and pepper. And, of course, the most popular fruit of all . . ."

Limpet blew out his cheeks in relief that there would be some normal fruit ice cream after all.

". . . tomato!" Mum declared. "The *best* tomato ice cream anyone has ever tasted!"

Eve was making a tower of tuna tins on the floor. It was almost up to her chin.

"How about vanilla?" asked Limpet.

"Limpet, there are oceans of raspberry ripple, mountains of rocky road, too many tutti fruttis . . ." said Mum, waving a giant, floppy mushroom about.

"People like tutti frutti," mumbled Limpet, even if he just liked vanilla.

"People can get those ice creams everywhere," Mum said as the mushroom flapped back and forth on its long stem. "But they can't get *these* ice creams." She waved the mushroom with one last flourish. The top of it fell off. A seagull dashed in through the door, knocking over Eve's tuna tower, and grabbed the morsel from the floor, before quickly waddling out again.

"But . . ." Mum smiled at Limpet. ". . . I did buy some vanilla pods especially for you to make your own ice cream."

Limpet didn't feel like making ice cream right now. He was still thinking about chickens and kids with blue tongues and a tooth on the blue tongue and Mr Fluffy and being CRUSHED and Things That Might Go (Badly) Wrong.

He had already written a new list of Things That Have Gone (Badly) Wrong:

1. A freaky chicken.
2. A rocket tooth.
3. Mr Fluffy wanting to CRUSH everything.
4. Ice creams that I know will taste like bins or fish heads, or fish heads taken out of bins, or worse.

He needed something to go right for him. He needed something to take away these worries that bubbled in his tummy. He needed a change of luck.

He remembered that the lemon was still in his pocket. The lemon that had rolled up to his foot.

He felt it and that little fizz ran through his hand again. It was as if the fruit was trying to tell him something.

Norman had called it a lucky lemon. Could that be true?

Of course it couldn't.

But maybe he should test out the lemon anyway. Just to see.

But what if it went wrong? What if it was a poison lemon? Or a lemon with some kind of lemon worm inside? Or a lemon that made his head explode like the cola-and-mints boy?

Limpet needed someone to test the lemon on. He looked at Eve. Eve picked her nose.

Nah. He wouldn't care if her head exploded, but what if she got very lucky instead? He wouldn't be able to stand that.

"*Awk*," said the mushroom-stealing seagull as it waddled past the door. Limpet had an idea.

Chapter 12

Splottpool's promenade was quiet apart from two girls who were kicking a football a short distance away.

Limpet watched the seagull pecking at the bin around the side of the shop.

His mum had put bags of dirty and spilled sweets in the bin, tying them up carefully first. The seagull peck-peck-pecked at the narrow gap at the top of the bin, but couldn't get the tasty goodies inside.

Limpet pressed a hole in the lemon and squeezed a little juice on to a mushroom. Then a bit more juice. Then another drop, just for good measure.

He put the soggy mushroom on the ground

and stepped back. The seagull didn't see it and kept pecking at the bin.

The girls were still playing football, laughing as they kicked the ball between them. Further away, someone was skateboarding up the promenade in the shop's direction. It was the hairy man who used to own the shop, his eyebrows blowing around the edges of his helmet.

How would Limpet get the bird's attention?

"Awk?" he guessed.

"*Awk?*" said the seagull, looking up.

"Awk," said Limpet, pointing at the mushroom.

"*Awk,*" said the seagull, and it came over and nibbled on the lemony mushroom. Its face screwed up. It sneezed. It shook its head. It coughed and flapped its wings and coughed some more. The mushroom must have tasted *horrible.*

The seagull ate the rest of it anyway, tipping back its head and gulping it straight down. Nothing happened – apart from the seagull shaking its head and waggling its beak and looking exactly like anyone would look if they had just eaten a lemon-soaked mushroom.

"Watch out!" one of the footballers shouted. She had kicked the ball straight into the path of the hairy man.

The ball hit the back of his skateboard and bounced high. The skateboard flipped up under his feet. He jumped in the air, spun, grabbed the skateboard and slid across the top of a bench. Seeing the ball falling from the sky, he headed it straight at Limpet.

Limpet dodged it but fell over.

The ball hit the wall behind him and knocked against the bin. The bin wobbled . . . wobbled some more . . . and fell over. The bag of old sweet treats fell at the seagull's feet. The ball landed on the bag, bursting it with a POP.

Sprinkles and chocolate dust exploded all over the seagull.

It greedily ate every sweet it could, swallowing cola bottles in one go, throwing marshmallows high in the air so it could catch them on the way down. It was in some sort of seagull sweet heaven.

Whoah, thought Limpet. *That was lucky for the seagull.*

No, that was *more* than lucky. That was the luckiest thing Limpet *had ever seen.*

Norman had been right. The lemon must be magic after all.

Standing up, Limpet realised he had sat on the squeezed lemon when he fell over. His tracksuit trousers were wet with the juice.

He wondered if he should suck his trousers for luck? No, he didn't want to suck his trousers.

But he *did* want that good luck. He would need another lucky lemon. *Loads* more lucky lemons.

There was only one place to find them.

Chapter 13

Limpet liked zebra crossings. And traffic wardens. And pressing the button on the traffic lights and waiting until it was green. And . . . well, he liked all the safe, not-at-all-dangerous ways to cross a road.

But there was no safe way to cross the busy road to the little garden on the fairy fort roundabout. Cars and bikes zoomed in either direction, swerving to avoid the jungly circle plonked right in the middle.

Norman didn't seem so worried about the traffic. "Go on Curtis, good girl," said Norman, releasing the chicken.

The bird flapped her scrawny wings and rose above the cars and a very surprised cyclist before disappearing into the roundabout garden.

A woman about Limpet's granny's age popped up in the tall grass. With thick gardening gloves, she pushed up the brim of her wide sunhat to see where the chicken had come from.

"Norman!" she shouted. "And a not-Norman!"

"That's Mrs Cricket," Norman told Limpet.

Mrs Cricket shuffled to the shed squeezed in the middle of the roundabout. It didn't look big enough for even half a person to fit in, yet Mrs Cricket disappeared into it, rustling noisily inside before returning with what looked like a rolled-up bit of carpet.

Pushing through the greenery to the edge of the roundabout she whipped out the carpet and it unfurled across the road.

The carpet was a furry zebra crossing and cars screeched to a stop either side of it. Limpet and Norman hurried across the black and white

striped carpet.
As soon as they
stepped into the long
grass, stalks and leaves at
the edge of the roundabout,
Mrs Cricket pulled the furry zebra
crossing back after them.

"Hello, Norman," she said.

"Hi, Mrs Cricket. We found one of your
lemons," said Norman. "Well, Limpet found it."

"It's Liam," said Limpet, telling her his real
name as he showed her the squashed lemon.

Mrs Cricket looked at the mushy yellow fruit. "Oh no, that's not Liam the lemon," she said. "Liam is much yellower. This lemon was Jeff."

"No, I didn't mean that—" said Limpet, but Mrs Cricket kept talking.

"Anyway, you can keep that lemon. It must have tried to run away. They always do that if they get too ripe. Now, you'd better come in before the daisies bite your ankles." Limpet looked down at the daisies. They looked like normal daisies. Not bitey daisies. He walked in quickly, just in case.

Pushing through the dense grass and broad leaves, Limpet couldn't believe what he saw on the other side.

Chapter 14

The garden was *so* much bigger on the inside than it looked from the outside.

The roundabout wasn't even round – it was somehow a wide square, bursting with life. Fruits, leaves, berries and nuts of every colour spilled out everywhere. Purple and yellow, orange and white, red and black. All this colour and life almost made Limpet dizzy.

The wooden shed at the centre was rickety and rotting. Tools spilled out of its door. Low, neat rows of leafy plants stretched towards a wall of tall stalks and thick trees around the edges.

To their right were low plastic tunnels through which Limpet could see the silhouettes

of plants. They seemed to move and squirm inside.

To their left was a busy beehive, with insects coming and going. It was far enough away that

Limpet didn't need to worry about the bees. But he worried about them anyway.

"Are those . . . bananas?" he asked, looking at the bendy fruit on one exotic tree.

"Sort of," said Mrs Cricket, pulling one from the tree and peeling it. "They talk a lot more than normal bananas. And, as you know, normal bananas won't shut up at the best of times. I call them blah-blah-nanas, which I'm sure you'll agree is *hilarious*."

She bit into the banana. The banana didn't say anything.

"What are those red, spiky fruits?" Limpet asked, pointing at a small bush.

"They're like cranberries, but much smarter," said Mrs Cricket, now feeding seeds to a happy Curtis. "They're such know-it-alls, but very good to eat the night before a big exam."

"What do they taste like?" asked Limpet.

"Do you know what a raspberry tastes like?" she asked.

"Yes," said Limpet.

"Well, they taste nothing like that," she said.

Mrs Cricket showed them around the garden.

"Those pears over there make you invisible."

"Invisible?" said Limpet.

"Well, you're invisible as long as no one looks at you," said Mrs Cricket. "And those blueberries make you scared of everything. Or they make you scary. It's one or the other. I suppose you could call them boo-berries. Get it?"

She waited for the boys to laugh, so Limpet laughed to make her happy but it sounded like a snort and he was sorry he did it.

"Also, never eat those peanuts over there unless you want to go to the toilet," she said. "And I mean, go to the toilet a *lot*."

"I told you the fruit here was magic," said Norman.

"Is this really a fairy fort?" asked Limpet.

"It is," said Mrs Cricket, sitting in a low deckchair by the shed and scooping some seeds from a bag to feed Curtis. "The fairies built it a long time ago, way before Splottpool was here. A fairy fort is a special place. If anyone destroys one, they are cursed to a terrible life for ever."

"For ever?" asked Limpet, worried about stepping on something and breaking a bit of the fairy fort.

"FOR EVER!" said Mrs Cricket sternly. Then she relaxed again. "Or maybe a week. The fairies don't like to tell you what they'll do. They just do it."

Limpet thought he saw a fairy in the grass, moving carefully around the stones. But it was just a woodlouse. "Can we . . . see the fairies?" he asked.

"Oh no, you won't see them!" laughed Mrs Cricket.

"Is that because the fairies are invisible?" asked Limpet.

"Ha ha no, don't be silly," said Mrs Cricket. "Invisible fairies? That would be *crazy*."

Limpet felt a bit silly for asking.

"No, it's Sunday," said Mrs Cricket. "The fairies have gone to play bingo."

"Fairies play bingo on Sundays?" asked Limpet.

"Of course not!" Mrs Cricket laughed again. "They usually have their ninja class on Sundays, but it was cancelled this week."

Limpet was *very* confused.

"Fairy forts have magical soil," she said, clapping her hands so the last seeds fell at the grateful Curtis's feet. "And all the feelings and hopes and dreams and worries of the people of Splottpool feed into the soil too. And then, to make it extra special, we add one final, incredible, *sensational* ingredient."

"Fairy dust?" asked Limpet, picking up what looked like an apple.

"Horse poo," said Mrs Cricket. "The plants love it!"

Limpet put the apple down again.

"I heard the lemons are lucky," said Norman. "Limpet gave it to a seagull and a bin exploded all over the seagull. Or something."

"*Buk*," said Curtis. Mrs Cricket petted the scrawny chicken.

"Oh those lemons give you luck all right," she said.

"Can Limpet have some more lemons? He needs lots of luck right now," asked Norman.

Mrs Cricket adjusted the brim of her sunhat and shook her head. "No. Not a chance. There is not a single hope in a million years that I can give you one of these highly powerful lemons, or may I be struck down by a terrible plague of—"

"He needs the lemons to defeat Mr Fluffy," said Norman, mischievously.

"How many do you need?" Mrs Cricket asked, jumping up from the deckchair and

scaring Curtis the chicken as she marched
straight for the lemon tree.

Norman grinned at Limpet. "Mrs Cricket
doesn't like Mr Fluffy."

"That man tried to crush this garden," she said while plucking lemons from the tree. "He wanted to destroy it. He wanted to poison the soil with gone-off ice cream and then build a shop here."

"He wants to crush my mum's new ice cream shop," said Limpet. "And it's all my fault."

"That man is always up to something," she said, selecting the juiciest, lemoniest lemons on the tree. "If there's anybody the fairies would most like to use their ninja skills on, it's Fluffy." She handed a pile of lemons to Limpet, who couldn't hold them all so carefully put a couple in his armpits.

Mrs Cricket grabbed the rolled-up zebra crossing and walked them back out of the peaceful garden, through the high plants and to the edge of the noisy road again.

"Now, before you use those lemons, there are three very important things you *must* remember," she said. "Whatever you do—"

GGGRRRROOOMMMMMMMMMM!
A truck went by, its engine so loud Limpet
didn't hear what Mrs Cricket said.

". . . Number two, you absolutely must make
sure to—"

ZZZZEEEEEEEEEEE!! A motorbike
zoomed past, drowning out her words.

". . . and third and most important of all: Do.
Not—"

BBRRAAAMMMMMMMMM!!!
BBEEEEEEPPPPPP!!! The truck honked at
the motorbike and the motorbike beeped back
and Limpet couldn't hear anything else.

"Anyway," said Mrs Cricket. "I'm sure none of
that will be a problem. Good luck!" She unrolled
the zebra crossing across the road.

As he and Norman stepped on to it, Limpet
was sure he felt something nip at his ankles.
Looking down, he saw a daisy turn away as if
pretending it hadn't tried to bite anyone.

Chapter 15

Limpet didn't have much time. Tomorrow was the first day at his new school. His mum's ice cream shop would open at the end of the week. He needed all the luck in the world. To make everything A-OK for his mum. And for himself.

He knew what he had to do. He had to be brave. He had to make ice cream. Not vanilla ice cream, but magical ice cream. Impossible ice cream. Lucky lemon ice cream. (He would put in a little bit of vanilla just to be safe.)

He laid the lemons on the kitchen counter in his new house in his new town, feeling the little zap of luck through his hands when he touched them. And even though he worried – even though he worried *a lot* – he tried to ignore that

voice in his tummy telling him that so much
could go wrong.

How much lemon juice should he put in?
Mrs Cricket said they brought luck. He wanted
lots of luck. He wanted to be super lucky. So he
put every last drop of juice from every single
lemon into the ice cream and made a big batch
of lemony ice cream to freeze and eat the next
day. His *lucky* day.

Chapter 16

Limpet woke the next morning, on the top bunk in the new bedroom he was sharing with his sister.

It would be his first day at the new school, but that was not his first thought. His first thought was this: *Must. Eat. Ice. Cream.*

His next thought after that was: *Even. Though. It's. Not. Vanilla. Ice. Cream.*

Then he thought one more thing: *Eve. Talks. In. Her. Sleep. She. Is. So. Evil.*

Swinging his legs off the bed, Limpet dropped down and landed on one of Eve's toy cars. Yelping, he staggered back and sat on his sleeping sister's belly.

Eve shot up and hit her head on the top bunk. "You punched me in my sleep!" she cried.

Limpet hopped, holding his sore foot. "*Your* toy attacked my foot!"

"*You* snore really loudly!" said Eve.

"*YOU* talk all night in your sleep," he said. "To unicorns!"

"Your *feet* smell!" Eve said.

"Your **ALL OF YOU** smells!" Limpet said.

"You smell of lemons," she said.

He did smell of lemons.

"You smell of . . . of . . . stinky!" he said.

Mum walked in. "Limpet, don't call your sister stinky."

"But . . . !" He pointed at the car-shaped mark on the sole of his foot.

"There's an awful smell of stinky feet in here," said Mum. "And lemons."

Well, this was *not* the sort of start Limpet had wanted. On a Monday. On his first day at a new school.

At breakfast, he hurriedly ate his porridge and started to worry about something else. He wrote in his notebook:

THINGS THAT MIGHT HAPPEN IF THE ICE CREAM MAKES ME TOO LUCKY

Bins of sweets will explode
   everywhere I go.
Money will start falling out of
   bank machines when I walk
   by.
I might never be given
   homework ever again.
I'll win all the raffles in the
   world.

So much luckiness might happen, but all Limpet wanted was enough luck to make his mum's ice cream shop a big success. And stop it being crushed. He wanted nothing more. Nothing less.

Except maybe to become super rich and famous. But that was all.

He would have thought about this some more

except that Eve opened her mouth to show off mushed-up porridge. "So evil," he said.

Finishing his breakfast, he took his spoon to the freezer and opened up the tub of freshly made, golden lemon ice cream. Icy lemon light sparkled on his face. Limpet scraped a sliver from the top and tasted the ice cream.

It was amazing.

He felt sparks inside him, just like he had felt them on his fingertips when he touched the lemon, but this time they ran from his chest to his shoulders and down to his toes and back up again. Was this good luck?

"We just won a prize," Mum said, walking into the room, laughing with disbelief and holding a raffle ticket high. "A dinner at the Golden Grub, the fanciest restaurant in Splottpool!"

They cheered. Eve spat porridge everywhere as she did.

Limpet couldn't believe it. That was *incredible*.

The good luck had arrived straight away, with just a *taste* of ice cream.

He shovelled more ice cream in, spoonful after spoonful until he was halfway through the tub and got a bolt of brain freeze so bad he worried his head might explode like that cola-and-mints boy.

While he was worrying about his brain exploding, his mother clapped her hands and shouted. "We're late for school!"

And that was the start of everything going (badly) wrong.

Chapter 17

The car wouldn't start. It wouldn't start even though Limpet's mum turned the key loads of times and called the car rude names and slapped the steering wheel and got out and stared at the car *very hard.*

Mum checked the engine before slamming the bonnet and sticking her head in the window to tell Limpet and Eve, "I can't fix it. We'll have to cycle."

They hurriedly put on their helmets and dragged their bikes out of the house. Limpet's schoolbag was so heavy with books he wobbled on the road.

He cycled through something scrunchy. Broken glass. *POP!* Air hissed from his tyre until it was flat.

"You're going to have to hop on the back of my bike," said Mum.

Limpet was ten. He was not six years old like Eve. He was not a baby. There was no way he would get on the back of Mum's big mummy bike. Not a chance. Never. Ever.

"No. No. No," he said. And then, in case he hadn't been clear, "No!"

"Ok then," said Mum. "You cycle Eve's bike and she can get on the back of mine."

"Yay!" said Eve.

"But . . ." said Limpet.

It was too late, Eve was already climbing up on Mum's bike.

He found out that there is only thing worse than being late for your first day at school – being on time for your first day at school while riding your little sister's bike. A bike so small Limpet's knees knocked his ears as he pedalled. A bike that had a back seat for a teddy. And

streamers flowing from the handlebars. And very loud clicking beads on its spokes so that everyone at the school gates turned to watch him.

Norman was parking his bike as Limpet arrived. He waved. Limpet waved back with some streamers stuck to his fingers. Limpet felt every single pair of eyes in the school watching him. He felt very sweaty. From cycling a little

bike with small but *very loud* wheels. And from eating too much lemon ice cream after breakfast.

But I'm lucky, thought Limpet. *This will get better. It will be a good day. A good week.*

It wasn't a good day. And it turned out to be the start of a bad week.

Here are five (Really) Bad Things that happened to Limpet that week . . .

Chapter 18

MONDAY'S BAD THING

The teacher, Miss Waite, welcomed Limpet to his new school. "Everyone, say hello to . . ." She checked the name on the roll call, ". . . Limpet Lewis?"

The kids laughed. Limpet shrank down in his seat. "It's – it's – it's Liam, Miss," he said.

"But his mum calls him Limpet," said Norman, sitting beside him. Norman was just trying to help. It didn't help at all.

"Has anybody met Limpet already? I mean, Liam, sorry!" asked Miss Waite. They all put their hands up.

"How do you all know Liam-pit?" said Miss

Waite. The whole class laughed again. "I mean Liam. So sorry again. I don't know what's got into me."

"We saw him on his funny bike," said a girl.

"We saw the ice cream chicken stuff," said a boy.

"Ha ha, Liam-pit," said another.

Limpet really wanted to climb out of the window and run away and live in a cave or something so he would never have to talk to anyone again.

Miss Waite could see he wasn't happy. "Well, let's all welcome Limpet . . . I mean *Liam*. Everyone together now . . ."

The whole class chanted their welcome. "*WELCOME-TO-THE-CLASS-LIMPET . . . WE-MEAN-LIAM*."

TUESDAY'S BAD THING

Limpet had another spoonful of lemon ice cream at breakfast. He felt that fizz of lemony luck inside him again.

A short while after school began, he lifted his schoolbag but didn't notice that it was upside-down until far too late. His books poured on to the floor. His pencil case too, which was open and spilled pencils and pencil shavings everywhere.

His snack fell out too, his apple rolling across the floor, between the tables, right to the end of the room where it knocked over a broom. The falling broom clipped the bookshelf. The books fell like dominoes, one after another, until reaching the end of the shelf where *The Big Encyclopaedia Of Monsters And Myths* fell on the cage holding Carrots, the class hamster. The cage flipped into the air. It landed with a crash.

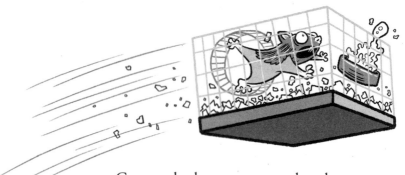

Carrots the hamster escaped and
ran up a boy's trouser leg. The whole class
went *crazy*.

While everyone was busy looking for
Carrots the hamster up their schoolmate's leg,
Limpet looked again at the open window and
wondered if he might run away and find that
cave to live in.

WEDNESDAY'S BAD THING

Limpet had another spoonful in the morning.
Felt the ice cream buzz inside him. Surely his
luck would change. It *had* to change.

It was raining after school so his mother came
to collect him. This was good luck at last. Until

he opened the door and saw two children's car seats inside. Eve was already in one. She smiled a very evil smile.

"I'm not sitting in that seat in front of everyone," said Limpet.

"I couldn't find a booster seat so I used your old toddler seat," said Mum. "It's only for a few minutes. And it's the law. If the police see you, you might to go to jail. And I'm sure you don't want to go to jail."

"*I* want Limpy to go to jail," said Eve.

Limpet bit his lip and gave his mum a look that told her he wasn't stupid and knew he wouldn't go to jail for that. Well, he was *sort of* sure he wouldn't go to jail.

He imagined himself sitting in a jail cell in a stripy uniform with a ball and chain around his ankle until he grew a really long beard. A long beard would look silly on a ten-year-old.

The rain bounced off Limpet's hood and ran down his nose. He had no choice. He squeezed into the seat. He pulled his jacket hood over his head as they drove away. At least the window was up and the rain drops meant no one could see in. Until Eve rolled down her window and let *everyone* see in.

"Bye, Limpet-I-mean-Liam," his schoolmates called.

THURSDAY'S BAD THING

When he looked in the freezer the ice cream was gone. His mother had put the container in the dishwasher. Limpet groaned.

"You'll never guess what happened," Mum said, busying about the house. "Eve emptied the dishwasher and found money inside. How lucky is that?!"

This wasn't fair. Even the dishwasher was

99

luckier than him.

If there was no ice cream left, what else could he do?

He had an idea. A bad idea. But it would have to do.

Limpet would have to suck his trousers.

THURSDAY'S OTHER BAD THING

He had put his tracksuit trousers in a pile of dirty clothes in the corner of his room. He pulled them out, peeling a dirty sock off one of the legs.

He could still smell the lemon on the pocket of his trousers, from where he had fallen and squashed it.

Pulling the pocket inside out, he saw fat seeds and bits of lemon mush. It had almost all dried in but there was a still a tiny bit of juiciness.

Closing one eye and trying not to breathe or

smell anything, he reluctantly stuck out the tip of his tongue. He licked his trousers. What did his trousers taste like? They tasted like sweaty socks and dirty tracksuit trousers and just the tiniest, teensiest bit of lemon.

And even though Limpet so wanted to be lucky, he knew that licking smelly tracksuit trousers was *not* something lucky people did.

So there you have it. Those are five (Really) Bad Things that happened to Limpet that week.

Oh, hold on. While we were reading about the five (Really) Bad Things that happened to Limpet that week, a sixth (Really) Bad Thing happened to Limpet that day.

His leg fell off.

Chapter 19

FRIDAY'S BAD THING

Oh, wait, *Limpet's* leg didn't fall off.

The leg of his *chair* fell off while he was sitting at home writing the list of Things That Have Gone (Badly) Wrong in his notebook. It collapsed and he fell, hurting his leg a little bit and his bottom a bigger bit.

Worse than all of that, Eve was there when the chair broke. She laughed. And laughed. And choked a bit on her rice cake, spraying crumbs all over Limpet. Then she laughed again and laughed and choked and laughed and coughed and laughed.

As he sat on the ground, with a sore backside

and very hurt pride, he could still feel the spark of the lemon's magic deep down inside him. It hadn't gone away. But why had it not worked? Why had it brought him only *bad* luck?

His mum's shop opened *tomorrow*. He was running out of time to stop Mr Fluffy crushing her dreams. It would be his fault.

This was bad. Very bad.

The doorbell rang. *What now?* thought Limpet.

Chapter 20

A tall girl about his age stood at the door, with a smile that beamed so much her cheeks pushed her eyes closed.

She wore a uniform – yellow jumper, red trousers and a red and yellow striped scarf knotted around her neck. She was covered from her waist to her neck in metal badges, each shaped like a shield with a little picture on it. There were so many badges that when she moved, even a little, she sounded like a big bag of tin cans.

"Hi," she said. "I'm Amelia. Do you like Brussels sprouts?"

Before Limpet could even answer such a strange question, Norman and Curtis the chicken appeared from behind Amelia. "We've come to help," said Norman. "Amelia does lots of stuff."

"*Some* stuff," said Amelia.

"And things," said Norman.

"A few things," said Amelia.

"She does rugby, painting, golf, football, chess, writing classes, piano classes, Korean, golf – did I already say golf? Anyway she does *everything*."

"Not all at the same time," said Amelia, her badges clattering and clanging against each other.

"*Buk*," said Curtis, getting a fright.

"What uniform is that?" Limpet asked her.

"The Super Troupers," she said.

"They're kind of like the scouts and guides and beavers and cubs all put together. But superer," said Norman.

Limpet wondered how she managed to stand up straight with all that metal hanging from her. It must have weighed more than an elephant. More than an elephant made of metal.

"What's that badge for?" asked Limpet, pointing at one with a little picture of scissors on it.

"That's my Haircutting badge," said Amelia.

"And that one?" asked Limpet pointing at one with a picture of a dog.

"That's my Taking Care of Puppies badge."

"And that?"

"That's my Giving Puppies Haircuts badge." She smiled, rattling a bit. "Norman said your mum is opening the ice cream shop," she said.

"Yeah. It's opening tomorrow," said Limpet.

"She's making spaghetti ice cream," said Norman.

"Cool," said Amelia, even though Limpet knew it wasn't cool at all.

"And Norman said you had a lucky lemon from the fairy fort."

Limpet nodded. "I had lots of lemons. In ice cream. I don't think it worked. I think it made everything worse."

"Carrots the hamster went up someone's leg!" said Norman, like it was one of the most amazing things he had *ever* seen. Which it was.

"I just wanted to be lucky so we could stop Mr Fluffy from crushing Mum's ice cream shop," said Limpet.

"Amelia can help because she has a Science badge . . ." Norman pointed at one on Amelia's shoulder. He turned Amelia around – her whole body seemed to shake. There were more badges underneath her backpack. Norman pointed to another one. "And a Maths badge."

"Using science and maths, we can test if you're lucky or unlucky," Amelia told Limpet.

"How do we do that?" asked Limpet.

"Through the magic of science," she smiled and punched the air, all the badges rattling like a suit of armour. "And Brussels sprouts."

Chapter 21

Amelia had a question before they carried out the experiments. The Worst Question in the World. "Why are you called Limpet?" she asked.

"It doesn't matter," said Limpet.

"Is it to do with seashells?" she asked.

"No," said Limpet.

"Did you have a limp when you were smaller?" asked Norman.

"No," said Limpet. He was not telling anyone. Ever.

"*Buk-bawk*," said Curtis.

"I prefer Liam anyway," he said.

"Ok, Limp— Liam," said Amelia, reaching into her backpack, her badges rattling. She pulled out a tall, colourful chocolate box. "So, *do* you like Brussels sprouts?"

"No way!" said Limpet. "They taste like tiny cabbages that have been soaked in burps. You would have to be crazy to like Brussels sprouts."

"I *love* Brussels sprouts!" said Norman, excited.

Amelia showed Limpet the chocolates piled up in the box. Their wrapping was so gold it reflected a warm glow on his face. His mouth watered.

"I saw this prank online," said Amelia. "Someone wrapped loads of Brussels sprouts in chocolate wrappers to fool their dad."

Amelia rolled up her sleeves, badges and all, and shook the box. "Don't worry, there are twenty chocolates in the box," said Amelia. "Only one Brussels sprout is wrapped up and pretending to be a chocolate. So, you'll probably pick a chocolate. Go on. Pick one."

Limpet shuffled the chocolates around like he

was picking a raffle ticket before pulling out a
golden-wrapped ball.

"Open it," Amelia said.

He opened it slowly. "It's the Brussels sprout,"
he said.

"Yum," said Norman.

"Oh," said Amelia. "That might be just a

one-off, so science says you need to do it again to see if there's a pattern."

Turning her back so Limpet couldn't see, Amelia wrapped the Brussels sprout again, put it back in the box, and mixed all the chocolates up, before asking Limpet to choose a second time.

He picked the Brussels sprout. Again.

"Whoah," said Amelia.

"Scrummy," said Norman.

"Are you sure they're not all Brussels sprouts?" asked Limpet.

"No," she said. "Look." She offered Norman the box and he grabbed a wrapped ball, and groaned in disappointment as he opened it. "It's a chocolate. I was really hoping it would be the Brussels sprout."

"Let's try one more time," said Amelia. "This time, close your eyes so we know you can't see in the box and just pop the chocolate into your mouth."

Limpet did this, eyes squeezed shut as he picked one and unwrapped it into his mouth. *Please be chocolate. Please be chocolate. Please be chocolate.* It was the Brussels sprout.

"Ugghhh," he said, mouth filled with green, mushy stuff that tasted like old slippers.

"Not fair!" said Norman.

"I have a spare Brussels sprout, Norman," said Amelia, pulling it from her pocket and chucking it at Norman.

"Brilliant!" he said, throwing it straight into his mouth like a gobstopper. "It tastes like boiled socks, but tasty boiled socks."

Limpet couldn't believe it. He was unlucky. *Amazingly* unlucky. The most unlucky person ever. "But the lemon was supposed to be *lucky*," he said, sadly.

"Maybe we should follow the rules Mrs Cricket gave us," said Norman, picking a bit of Brussels sprout from between his teeth.

"What were they again?"

Limpet tried to remember what she had said. "What was first?" he wondered. "Oh, she said that whatever we do . . ."

"Blah, blah, something, something?" said Norman.

Limpet thought of the next thing. "Number two, she said we absolutely must make sure to . . ."

"Ehm . . . do *this* thing or *that* thing?" said Norman.

"And third and most important of all," said Limpet. "She said, 'Do. Not . . .'"

"*Buk-bawk,*" said Curtis the chicken.

This was no help at all.

"Maybe too many lemons are dangerous," said Amelia. "Or maybe you put them in the wrong food, or with the wrong ingredients. There are many reasons and we could run experiments. Science will tell us."

Limpet couldn't wait for science to help him. He needed to turn his luck around *now*. Before it was too late. It was time to visit the only person who would know how.

Chapter 22

Mrs Cricket flopped the furry zebra crossing across the busy road and Limpet, Amelia and Norman pushed their bikes across while annoyed drivers waited. Curtis was in a basket on the front of Norman's bike.

"Did you see any crab apples?" Mrs Cricket asked them as they reached the tall plants and grass on the edge of the roundabout. "Small apples? They roll sideways?" They shook their heads.

"Oh well, come on in!" she said. "Watch out for the daisies. They're *very* moody today." They followed her, checking for daisies on the way.

"Are the fairies here?" Limpet asked.

"Ah no," said Mrs Cricket. "There are no

fairies here." Limpet felt let down. There must be no fairies after all.

"It's Friday. They do their cheese-making class on a Friday. They make a great one that smells like the world's worst toilet. But it tastes *fantastic*. Speaking of which, how is your ice cream shop coming along, Liam?"

Limpet was so surprised to be called Liam that at first he didn't know Mrs Cricket was talking to him. "It's opening tomorrow," he said.

"You don't seem happy about it," said Mrs Cricket.

"I made ice cream with the lucky lemons and I feel their sparkiness inside me still," he said. "But I've had no luck. No luck at all."

"Did you follow the rules?" she asked.

"Yes!" said Norman.

"Really?" asked Mrs Cricket.

"No," said Norman. "We forgot them."

"I think I can see what's happened here," said Mrs Cricket. "What did you hope the lemons would give you?"

"Luck," he said.

"Exactly," she said.

"But I've had bad luck," he said. "Terrible luck. The worst luck."

"Really?" said Mrs Cricket. "It sounds like you've had a *lot* of luck."

"A lot of *awful* luck," said Limpet. "When will it wear off?"

Mrs Cricket looked around, and seemed to be thinking deeply about something. "How many lemons did I give you? There were some lemons in your hands. Some in your armpits. Did you have one in your ear?"

Limpet shook his head. No lemons fell out of his ear when he did.

"If my calculations are correct," she continued, "then the luck of those lemons will probably be totally gone by . . ." She licked her finger and stuck it in the air, ". . . tomorrow."

I really wish I hadn't eaten those lemons, thought Limpet.

"Come this way," said Mrs Cricket and walked through the high plants to the centre of the garden and the deckchair near the messy shed.

Bees buzzed in and out of the hive. Plants seemed to squirm inside the plastic tunnels. The colours all around made the day seem a hundred times brighter than it was. Mrs Cricket sat in her deckchair, gripping each side tight as she did. Then she pointed at an upside-down bucket beside her. "Sit down, young man," she said.

While Norman and Amelia examined the plants and flowers, and Curtis pecked at the grass, Limpet sat carefully on the bucket, worried it would crumple beneath him at any moment. But it felt strong.

Mrs Cricket lifted two apples from the ground and held one in each hand. "Do you know what's special about these apples?" she asked.

"Do they fly?" Limpet asked.

"No," she laughed. "They just lie there, like any old apples. And when I find them, they might be fresh from the tree, or they might have been lying there for a while." She seemed to weigh each apple in her hand. "But they both look like apples, right?"

Limpet nodded. They both looked just like apples. Nothing more. Nothing less.

"And they both taste like apples," she said, handing one to Limpet and encouraging him to take a bite. Limpet chewed and swallowed the delicious piece of apple.

"Sometimes one apple will taste as sweet as you could wish . . ." Mrs Cricket handed Limpet the second apple. He bit into it and wanted to spit it out straight away. It tasted *bad*.

". . . but the one that has been lying on the ground too long will taste bitter," she said. "Still, they're both apples. Do you understand?"

"Two apples?" he said.

"Exactly! Good lad," she said, standing up quickly. "Now if you don't mind, I'll have to say goodbye to you all. I have worms to plant."

They were soon on the furry zebra crossing again. "Remember," said Mrs Cricket, waving goodbye, "apples are apples."

Crossing the road, Limpet remembered something. "But what were the rules?" he called back.

"It's very simple," said Mrs Cricket. "Just—"

VVVVRRRROOOMMMMMMMM!

A very noisy truck went past, drowning out Mrs Cricket's advice.

". . . I hope that helps," she said, and disappeared back into the garden.

"That was great," said Amelia, upbeat. "What was she talking about?"

Limpet had no idea. No idea at all.

Oh, he *tried* to understand it all the way back home. It sounded like a story he was supposed to figure out. But he didn't want stories he was supposed to figure out.

He wanted a simple answer to his unlucky lemon problem. He wanted Mrs Cricket to tell him that all he had to do was put a special strawberry up his nose or wear shoes made out of awesome orange skin . . . or whatever it was.

He couldn't figure out the apples thing. He stopped thinking about it only when they went over a bump on their bikes and Curtis nearly flew out with a "*Buk-BAWK.*"

Arriving back at his house, he heard a sound growing louder. It was an old-fashioned music-box tune, but it sounded sick. Like the music box had eaten too many Brussels sprouts. *Ting-a-ling-a-bluerghhh* . . . And there was also the *ching-ching* of a bicycle bell.

Limpet looked up. His mum was on a bike, cycling towards them, waving while Eve sat in a cart at the back. An ice cream cart.

Ling-a-lang-a-luuuurrppppp . . . went the tune. *Ching-ching!* went the bell.

Limpet just knew, there and then, that he was not hearing any old bicycle bell. He was hearing the Bicycle Bell of Even Worse Luck.

Chapter 23

The multi-coloured cart had "Impossible Ice Creams" written across the side. The "I" in "Impossible" was a cone with what might have been a green ice cream on top. Or a cabbage. Limpet couldn't tell which. A folded orange and white umbrella stuck up from the middle of the cart.

Mum pulled up, with Eve sitting in one half of the empty ice cream fridge. "Isn't it great!" said Mum. "Look at this . . ." She pressed a button. The umbrella snapped open, reflecting lovely orange and white all over the cart.

Amelia and Norman cheered. Curtis clucked loudly and flapped wildly in a spray of feathers. Eve clapped her hands while sticking

her tongue out at Limpet. "Mr Puffy—" said Limpet's mum.

"Fluffy," said Limpet.

"—can have his big ice cream van. We're going to have our ice cream bike. Our *impossible* ice cream bike."

Limpet sagged with embarrassment. Nobody else's mum was cycling around trying to sell weird ice creams – with an evil sister sitting in the back.

The ice cream shop opened tomorrow. All he could hope for now was that things wouldn't get any more embarrassing. That this was as bad as it would get.

It was *not* as bad as it would get.

"Up you go," Mum said to Limpet as Eve climbed out of the fridge.

"Up *I* go?" asked Limpet. "Into the fridge?"

"No," she laughed. "On to the bike. Take the cart for a ride. You can cycle it to the shop. I'll follow you soon. I've got to drive equipment there to get it ready for tomorrow's spectacular grand opening. Will you be there, kids?"

"Absolutely!" said Norman.

"Definitely!" said Amelia, her badges rattling.

I have to stop thinking things can't get more unlucky, thought Limpet, *because every time I think things can't get more unlucky they get more unlucky* straight away.

He needed to be more positive, but as he stood in front of the ice cream bike he couldn't help but think of all the Things That Might Go (Badly) Wrong.

The cart might escape. The umbrella might launch into the air and knock a helicopter out of the sky and the helicopter might fall on Limpet's head. And worst of all, he might be *seen* by people in Splottpool.

It was too late. Amelia and Norman were

already on their bikes, ready to cycle with him. Curtis was sitting comfortably in the basket.

"You have to stop worrying what other people think," Mum said quietly to him.

Limpet did worry what other people thought.

"You need to stop worrying about *everything*."

Limpet did worry about everything.

"If we just had vanilla every day, everyone and everything would be the same," said Mum. "There would be no colour. No wild ideas. No fun. This world needs fun now more than ever."

"But, Mr Fluffy . . ."

"Mr Fluffy has his shop. And we'll soon have ours."

"I'm worried we'll have no luck," Limpet said.

"Limpet, I believe that you can make your own luck," she said. "Now, hop on the bike and I'll see you at the shop."

Limpet's mum handed him his helmet. He was going to say he was glad it wasn't an ice cream shaped helmet, but then he thought, *Don't give Mum the idea of making you wear an ice cream shaped helmet. Or a helmet that tastes of ice cream.*

So he said nothing and just started cycling, while the cart played sickly music-box songs. *Ting-a-ling-a-LEURRRPPPPP . . . Bong-a-bong-a-BORRRKK . . .*

Chapter 24

The cart was heavy and hard to cycle. Every time Limpet stopped, Amelia and Norman had to wait for him to catch up.

When he cycled very slowly, the music-box ice cream tune sounded like it was ill. *Ting-a-ling-a-luuurrrgghhhhh-a-lang-long-aleeeuuurrrbbbb . . .*

When he did get the cart moving quickly, it would burst into song and was really quite jolly. But Limpet was not quite jolly. He was not jolly at all.

"Hi Limpet . . . I mean Liam!" waved some kids from his school when they saw him pass. Limpet wished he could climb into the ice cream fridge in the cart and hide from the world. Maybe he would freeze solid in there and not be woken for a thousand years, when this would all be over and aliens had invaded and didn't care about ice creams.

"Hi!" Norman and Amelia called back to everyone as they cycled ahead of Limpet.

Sitting in her basket, Curtis the chicken looked back under Norman's arm, staring at Limpet with her freaky chicken eyes.

"*Buk-BAWK,*" said Curtis as they went over a bump.

Tingaling-a-dinga-LANGLONG-a-dingdong, went the music of the cart as it went over the same bump. The cart swung around a bit and Limpet felt it jolt as if it might come loose and run away.

A trail of cars crawled behind him, wishing he would hurry up. He could not hurry up.

Someone honked their horn. "*Buk,*" said Curtis.

As they turned on to the promenade near the

ice cream shop, Limpet was so relieved that he would soon be able to stop cycling this embarrassing cart. Until he stopped being worried about that and started worrying about something else.

He heard a very bad sound. Disco music and a motorbike engine.

"Is that . . . ?" asked Norman.

"It sounds like . . ." wondered Amelia.

Mr Fluffy was beside the little ice cream shop.

He sat on a sleek motorbike with an incredible ice cream cart behind it. If there were such things as ice cream cart races around a motor racing track, this was the kind of cart that would win everything.

Mr Fluffy wore a blue jumpsuit covered in dazzling glitter ice creams, a long pink cape that flapped in the breeze

and a helmet with a row of chocolate flakes
sticking up along the top like a Mohican.

He revved the motorbike engine, and the
disco tune got louder and his cart's lights flashed
brighter.

Limpet could smell the ice cream. It was
incredible. He tried not to drool but he couldn't
help it and had to wipe his chin.

As Limpet neared the shop, Mr Fluffy lifted
the visor on his helmet. He growled almost as
loudly as his engine.

Chapter 25

Vruummm went Mr Fluffy's motorbike, parked at the edge of the promenade by the sloshing sea.

Clank-clank, went Limpet's bike.

Waah-waah-wacka-wacka-waah, went Mr Fluffy's music.

BLERUGHH-a-ting-a-lang-a-BLURALURGEM, went Limpet's cart's music.

Mr Fluffy stepped off his bike, with his cape fluttering on the breeze. Taking some leaflets from an ice cream tray full of them, he started handing them out to dog walkers and joggers, people pushing prams and kids on scooters.

"I know Mr Fluffy's ice cream smells like your

coop," Norman said to the chicken, "but you have to stay in the basket."

A leaflet blew in the breeze, floating and flying until it stuck to Limpet's face. He pulled it free and stopped the cart to read it.

MR FLUFFY'S
MEGA
EMPORiUM
OF **AMAZiNG** AND
SPECTACTULAR
iCE CREAMS

FREE iCE CREAM
SATURDAY
NO WEiRD iCE CREAMS!

DON'T GO TO THE NEW SHOP
UNLESS YOU WANT
iCE CREAM POiSONiNG

"What a very mean man," said Amelia.

"We need to stop him handing out leaflets," said Limpet. "He's going to CRUSH Mum's shop. Let's take the leaflets from his cart so he can't hand out any more."

Limpet pushed hard on the pedals to get there. *Tring-a-ding-a-BLEURRPPHHH.*

He speeded up. *Tring-a-bong-a-ling-a-LEURRPPP.*

He got too fast.

"Too fast!" said Mr Fluffy, pointing at Limpet.

"No chickens!" he said, pointing at Curtis and Norman.

"Free ice cream!" he said, handing leaflets to two men power-walking along the promenade.

Limpet couldn't stop because his heavy cart was pushing on his bike. He headed straight for Mr Fluffy's super motorbike cart.

Limpet hit a bump in the promenade. His bicycle jumped in the air a bit. His cart jumped in the air *a lot*. On landing, it came loose from the bike and rolled at Mr Fluffy's cart. *Ting-a-tong-a-ling-a-long!*

"Oh," said Limpet.

"Ooh," said Norman and Amelia.

"No!" shouted Mr Fluffy as the cart went by, gathering speed, its music getting faster and faster.

It hit Mr Fluffy's cart, knocking the motorbike over, splashing sauce and sprinkles everywhere, and sending the big pile of leaflets up into the air. The Splottpool breeze took them and carried them up, up, up and all across the town.

Mr Fluffy grabbed the bike just before it could fall over the edge of the promenade and, after nearly falling into the water himself, lifted everything the right way up again just in time for Curtis to flap in his face. She wanted the sauce that smelled like her chicken coop.

Mr Fluffy simply pulled the visor down on his helmet and, after slipping a bit on spilled sauce and sparkling sprinkles, sat on the seat of his motorbike.

Limpet, Amelia and Norman didn't laugh. They didn't scream. They just stared with their mouths wide open.

"I will CRUSH your shop like it's nothing more than a chicken nugget under my fist," Mr Fluffy said.

"Don't listen to the grumpy man, Curtis," said Norman, blocking the chicken's ears.

Mr Fluffy drove off, leaving behind a mess on the ground and a sky full of leaflets blowing all across Splottpool. Everybody would know there was free ice cream at Mr Fluffy's tomorrow. Nobody would come to Limpet's mum's shop. It was going to be a disaster.

It was going to be a disaster because Mr Fluffy made amazing, secret-recipe ice creams, not ice creams no one would eat. Not boiled underpants ice cream or sweaty armpits ice cream or whatever.

It was all going wrong and it couldn't get any worse, Limpet thought.

Then he thought, *Stop thinking it won't get worse, because then it always gets worse.*

As soon as he thought that, it got worse. It got as bad as it could get.

Limpet's mum arrived in her car. Eve, biting on a lollipop, stepped out of the car, walked up to Amelia and Norman and asked them The Worst Question in the World.

Chapter 26

THE WORST QUESTION
IN THE WORLD

"Do you want to know why Limpet's called
Limpet?"

Chapter 27

"Don't you dare," Limpet warned his evil little sister. Eve dared.

"When Limpet was a little boy, he never let go of Mum," she said.

"Stop it, Eve," said Limpet. Eve didn't stop it.

"He held on tight to her all of the day and all of the night and all of the times in between. My mum says he got even stickier to her after I was born."

"I'm going to tell them that you talk to unicorns in your sleep," warned Limpet.

"Unicorns," said Norman. "Cool."

It is not *cool*, thought Limpet.

"So they called him Limpet cos he was so sticky."

"Oh, like seashells on the rocks," said
Norman.

"I thought you must have had a limp or
something when you were younger," said Amelia.

"Me too," said Norman. "I was a bit confused
because you don't have a limp now. You just
have sprinkles and sauce stuck to your trousers."
Limpet did have sprinkles and sauce stuck to his
trousers. They must have splashed there when
Mr Fluffy's cart fell over.

"*Buk*," said Curtis. The chicken pecked at
Limpet's foot with her scrawny beak.

"It's a stupid nickname," said Limpet. "It's
babyish."

"No, it's not," said Amelia. "It's just a
nickname. My dad calls me by the nickname he
gave me as a baby. Guess what it is."

Limpet shrugged, because he didn't want to
say anything stupid.

"Mee-Mee," said Amelia. "Mee-Mee is my

nickname at home because that's how I
used to say my name before I could talk
properly."

"Mee-Mee!" laughed Norman. "That's what
I'm calling you every day from now on."

"Don't even think about it," laughed
Amelia.

"OK, Mee-Mee," said Norman.

"I bet you have a nickname too, Norman,"
she said, smiling.

"Yeah, I get called loads of things at home,"
said Norman. "When my brothers and sister
want to annoy me they call me Normal instead
of Norman. Or Norm. Or the Normster.
Or Nor*boy* – you know, instead of Nor*man*. Or
Featherbrain, because of Curtis."

"*Buk*," said Curtis, pecking on spilled
sprinkles before spitting them out with a sneeze
and a cough. Curtis didn't like the sprinkles.
Maybe she had thought they were sparkly seeds.

"But my mum calls me Sunshine," said Norman. "I kind of like it when she does that."

"Sunshine!" laughed Amelia.

"It's better than Mr Grumpy-Poos, which is what she sometimes calls my biggest brother. He is a real Mr Grumpy-Poos sometimes."

Eve laughed at this, because Eve always laughed at any word with 'poo' in it. Limpet and Eve didn't agree on many things, but they could both agree that 'poo' is just a funny word. "Poo!" giggled Eve.

Norman and Amelia laughed too. They laughed very loudly.

"You lot seem to be having a good time," said Mum, walking by with an armful of baked beans, sugar and cream.

"Poos!" roared Eve. And they all laughed again. Limpet couldn't help but laugh too. It was funny. 'Poo' was a funny word. Their nicknames were funny too.

Limpet laughed very hard. As he laughed, something hit him. It was not a chicken.

It was an idea.

Chapter 28

That night – the night before the Shop of Impossible Ice Creams would open – Limpet took out his notebook of Things That Might Go (Badly) Wrong.

He added a new thing, in BIG WRITING, to his list of Things That Have Gone (Badly) Wrong.

Eve told Norman and Amelia why I am called Limpet.

That was supposed to be The Worst Thing That Could Happen. The Most Embarrassing Thing That Could Happen.

But it wasn't The Worst Thing. Or The

Most Embarrassing Thing. Even though it was
A Bit Embarrassing. It wasn't The End of the
World Embarrassing, like Limpet had thought it
would be.

Why wasn't it The Worst Thing? Because
Norman and Amelia hadn't laughed at him.
They hadn't embarrassed him. They hadn't told
him he was a big baby with a big baby
nickname.

Instead, they had told him their silly
nicknames. And Limpet had laughed along with
them.

He had worried so much about his friends
finding out why he was called Limpet that he
hadn't stopped to think that maybe they
wouldn't think it was that bad at all.

He looked at the other things he had written
on his list of Things That Had Gone (Badly)
Wrong.

Arriving at school on his sister's bike? *Really*

embarrassing. But everyone in his new school had been nice to him all week anyway.

Carrots the class hamster crawling up someone's leg? OK, maybe it wasn't great. But everyone had talked about it being the funniest thing they'd seen ever in their whole lives. So that was good.

The ice cream shop? Limpet worried about the ice creams his mum was making. The strange ice creams. The impossible ice creams. The weird ice creams. But Mum was happy. And that should make Limpet happy.

His sister was still evil, but unless he swapped her for another, less evil, sister, he was stuck with her for now.

Yes, he had been very, very unlucky. Amazingly unlucky. The unluckiest anyone had ever been, probably in the history of the world. In the history of the whole *universe*. In fact, there probably hadn't even been dinosaurs as unlucky as him. And they had been squashed by a giant rock from space.

But in every unlucky thing he could now see something lucky. New friends. Nice classmates. A happy mum.

Maybe everything wasn't one hundred per cent A-OK, but a lot of things were pretty good.

He wondered if the lemons had brought him lots of luck after all – just that some of it was really bad luck, and some of it was really *good* luck.

Is this what Mrs Cricket had meant with the two apples story? Each looking the same but one being sweet and one being bitter? Except the apples were lemons. And the apples were also luck. And . . .

Limpet stopped thinking about the apples story because it was too confusing and made his brain feel wobbly.

Mum popped her head into his room. "I meant to tell you that I put your ice cream in a different container," she said.

"My lemon ice cream?" he asked.

"Yep. There was only a bit left. That's why I put the big container in the dishwasher and put your ice cream in a smaller one. It's at the back of the freezer." She left the room again.

Well, this was lucky. Or was it? It was hard to tell what was what any more.

And at that moment – as Limpet was wondering what was lucky and unlucky, and how much of it was about life, and how much of it was because of the lemons – he remembered that he was still worried about Mr Fluffy. And what had happened with his cart.

And how angry he was when the cart turned over and . . .

Limpet looked at the bottom of his trousers. He saw the sauce still splattered on them. He saw the sprinkles stuck to the sauce.

Hold on a minute, he thought. *That's not sauce. Or sprinkles.*

Limpet chewed on his pencil for a moment, then slapped his notebook down on the table and realised that with all that bad luck had come some *very* good luck.

That wasn't sauce or sprinkles on his trousers. They were clues to Mr Fluffy's super-secret recipe. And Limpet had just figured it out.

Chapter 29

It was Saturday. The big day. The day the Shop of Impossible Ice Creams would open. The day Mr Fluffy would crush it by giving away free ice creams.

Mr Fluffy stood at the door of his spectacular shop, on the outside of the giant shopping centre that cast a shadow over the town. Wearing a simple pink and yellow apron, and a disco hairnet over his shock of red hair, he announced to the queue of people outside: "Free ice cream."

"Free ice cream?" they asked. "What's the catch?"

"Only one catch," Mr Fluffy said seriously.

"What?" they asked.

"No chickens," he answered.

The customers laughed . . . but stopped when they saw that Mr Fluffy wasn't laughing. He wasn't laughing at all.

He turned the shop's sign from CLOSED to OPEN and the line of hungry, excited people followed him inside. But three kids and a chicken did not.

Limpet appeared from around the corner, where he had been hiding – and watching everything. Mr Fluffy had come to their little shop twice. Now it was time for Limpet to pay him a visit. He had a plan. A BIG plan. And he was very nervous about it.

"He's going to be so grumpy," said Norman behind him, holding Curtis under his arm. That was one problem Limpet was nervous about.

"And so mean," said Amelia, beside him. That was another problem.

"*Buk-bawk*," said Curtis. And the chicken was *definitely* a problem.

Limpet was nervous about having the chicken with them, but she was a BIG part of their BIG PLAN.

Amelia was in her Super Trouper's outfit again and rattled with excitement. Limpet closed his eyes, took a deep breath, and pulled the last of the lemon ice cream from his backpack. It was sludgy and soft, but he carefully drank from the corner of the tub and immediately felt the spark run through his body. A spark of luck.

It felt like a volcano of luck bubbling away inside him. Or like when he drank fizzy drinks too quickly and really needed to burp. Except he'd be burping luck. Good or bad luck, he wasn't sure. And he was so nervous he didn't want to think about burping anything right now. Even luck.

"I've something for you," said Amelia. She took a badge from her shoulder. It had a picture of a lion on it. "That's my Super Trouper's Bravery badge. I think you should have it."

Limpet pinned it to his chest and it made him happy – even though he worried that the sharp pin would poke his skin and cut him and make him bleed and faint.

He felt the lemon ice cream's luck bouncing around inside him. "Let's go," he said.

Chapter 30

Mr Fluffy's Mega Emporium of Amazing and
Spectacular Ice Creams looked mega. It smelled
amazing. It *was* spectacular.

Dazzling lights. Bright colours. Aromas that
made Limpet's mouth drool so much he started
to dribble.

Gleaming pink counters ran along either
side of the shop, and behind each were colourful
tubs of ice cream. Sparkling ice cream. Glowing
ice cream. Ice creams that looked like they'd
pop and crackle and have a big party in your
tummy.

And none of them had vegetables in them.

Limpet wanted one of those ice creams. Even
the not-vanilla ones. He wanted an ice cream so

badly – even though he knew the terrible secret of what was in them.

He needed to ignore the smells – the amazing smells – and the mega colours and the flood of drool in his mouth, and get to the front of the queue, where Mr Fluffy was handing out free ice creams without a smile.

Limpet, Amelia and Norman made their way up the queue. They pushed through the people leaving, slurping their free ice creams.

"Excuse me," they said.

"Sorry," they said.

"Yes, that's a real chicken," they said.

"*Buk-bawk*," said Curtis.

Limpet felt that last blast of lemony luck inside him, ready to burst out like mints in cola.

They neared the shiny pink counter. His hairnet flashing disco lights, Mr Fluffy was handing out free ice creams. "Next," was all he said as he scooped ice cream on to a cone and handed it grumpily to a customer.

Behind him were jars of sweets and sprinkles and sauces and what looked like delicious goodies of every colour and pattern. Pink striped goodies. Yellow sparkly goodies. Green gooey goodies.

"Next," said Mr Fluffy, giving away another ice cream. Limpet wiped the dribble from the corners of his mouth.

"Next," Mr Fluffy said. Then he saw who was next.

"You . . ." he growled at Limpet. "Them . . ." he snarled at Amelia and Norman. "That!" he snapped, pointing the pointy end of a cone at Curtis.

Everyone in the shop looked at Curtis the chicken. Curtis looked at Mr Fluffy with her freaky chicken eyes. "*Buk-bawk*."

Everyone looked at Mr Fluffy.

"No. Chickens," said Mr Fluffy. He scooped some golden ice cream out on to the cone, wafted it in front of Limpet's nose so the smell almost drove him crazy, and handed it over his head to a man standing behind him.

Mr Fluffy made a noise, a kind of "heh" that sounded halfway between a cough and choking. Limpet realised that was Mr Fluffy's laugh.

"Heh-heh," half-coughed, half-laughed Mr Fluffy again. He slowly scooped more ice cream, and gently placed it on top of a cone. Golden ice cream, that sparkled and glowed and looked like all the lost treasures of the world had been put into one single ice cream.

Its glow reflected on Limpet's face. It wasn't just mouthwatering, it was mouth*flooding*. Almost unbearable. He wafted it slowly in front of Limpet.

"You want the ice cream," said Mr Fluffy.

Limpet really *did* want the ice cream. He had

been hypnotised by how golden and sparkly it was, quite forgetting why he had come into the shop in the first place.

"*You* want it too," Mr Fluffy said, waving it at Amelia and Norman. Both of them stared at the ice cream with their mouths open and eyes swirling.

In his drool, Limpet tasted so much lemon, it made his eyes water. It shook him out of his trance. He remembered why he was there.

"I know your secret recipe!" Limpet shouted over the sound of slurping from all the people in the shop.

"*Gasp!*" said everyone in the shop, except for one man who almost choked on his tutti frutti.

"I saw sauce leaking from your van that day, but it didn't smell of sauce. It smelled of something else."

Limpet then did the oddest thing. He lifted up his leg and put his foot on the counter.

"No legs!" said Mr Fluffy. "No feet!"

Limpet ignored him and wobbled on one foot as he pointed at his tracksuit leg. "And yesterday, sauce and sprinkles splashed on my leg. But last night I found out that it's not sauce and sprinkles at all. Your secret is—"

"No talking!" said Mr Fluffy.

"You put paint and glitter in your ice cream," said Limpet.

People stopped slurping straight away.

"It's like the paint and glitter you give to little kids so they can do finger painting," said Amelia, pointing to a badge on her waist. "I know that because I have a Super Trouper Art badge. And, just to be sure, we did science tests on the sauce and sprinkles – because I have a Science badge." She pointed at the Science badge on her back.

"No badges!" said Mr Fluffy.

"*Ooooh*," said everyone in the shop.

"And the lovely smell?" said Limpet. "That's air fresheners. Like you get in toilets."

"*Eeurgh*," said everyone.

"No toilets!" said Mr Fluffy.

"That's why Curtis is always flapping to you," said Norman. "I use that air freshener in her chicken coop. It covers up the smell of chicken poo."

"No poo!" said Mr Fluffy.

Limpet giggled at the word 'poo'.

"No giggles!"

Everyone in the shop giggled.

"My ice creams are mega!" shouted Mr Fluffy. "My ice creams are amazing! My ice creams are spectacular!"

"Your ice creams are *weird*," said Norman.

"We think we can show everyone why," said Limpet. "You see, I thought I'd been really unlucky all week. Because I ate some lemons. They came from a roundabout. I turned them into ice cream and ate too many and got brain freeze and—"

"No blabbering!" said Mr Fluffy.

"Anyway, I had one last blast of luck left," said Limpet. "And I don't know if it will be good luck or bad luck. But my mum said you can make your own luck. And that's what I'm going to do. I'm going to make one big kaboom of luck."

"And one last kaboom of Curtis," said
Norman, letting go of the chicken. "Good bird.
Go find the nice smell."

Curtis flapped straight at Mr Fluffy. And
everything went CRAZY.

Chapter 31

Feathers flew. Jars fell. Ice creams spilled. The crowd screamed and gasped and screamed some more.

It went on like this for what seemed like *ages*, until, eventually, Curtis found a jar and stuck her head in it. She didn't peck or eat, she just calmed down and walked around with the jar on her head.

Another jar, filled with shiny red liquid, rolled across the floor to the feet of a woman.

SUPER STRAWBERRY SAUCE said the label, but it had curled at the corner. She peeled it off to reveal another label underneath. RED PAINT, said the real label.

"This *is* paint," said the woman.

"*Bleeeuurrgghh,*" said half the crowd in the shop.

Someone else picked up a jar of sprinkles and peeled that label off. "And these aren't sprinkles," they shouted. "It's ART GLITTER!"

"*Yeeeuuurrrghh!*" said the other half of the crowd.

Curtis waddled up to Limpet, who pulled the jar off the chicken's head. The label said NICE SWEETS, but Limpet peeled it away to reveal something written by hand in small writing.

CUT UP BITS OF AIR FRESHENER TO COVER UP THE SMELL OF PAINT AND MAKE ICE CREAM SMELL AND TASTE GOOD

"AAAAGHH!" shouted everyone. They spat out their ice creams. Dropped them. Flung them.

They had *not* been eating lovely, delicious ice creams, but paint, glitter, and tiny bits of air freshener – the kind used in toilets and chicken coops.

They tried to get out the door as quickly as they could, but stopped when Mr Fluffy called to them.

"I swear on the grave of my grandmother, Felicity O'Lump-McFluffy," he shouted. "There is no poison!"

Limpet picked a jar off the floor and peeled off the label to reveal the real label underneath:

POISON
(BANANA-FLAVOUR)

He held it up to show everyone.

The crowd ran again.

Chapter 32

Swept out with the crowd, Limpet, Amelia, Norman and Curtis the chicken walked away from Mr Fluffy's shop.

"It looks like Mr Fluffy's luck ran out," said Limpet.

"Oh, that's a cool thing to say," said Norman.

"Like something out of a film," said Amelia.

Limpet felt good but immediately wondered if this was one of those moments when things would suddenly get worse. But they didn't.

And he couldn't feel the spark inside him any more. The magic of the lucky lemons was gone in one big kaboom of luck.

So they walked on, towards the promenade. It was time for the grand opening of the Shop of Impossible Ice Creams.

Chapter 33

The ice cream shop looked different. Very different.

Limpet's mum had put chairs and small tables outside, where Limpet, Norman and Amelia now sat. An orange and white awning stretched from the shopfront. It flapped gently in the breeze.

IMPOSSIBLE ICE CREAMS

was written in lights across the side of the shop.

A cloth was draped across a blackboard by the door, but Limpet could see TODAY'S SPECIALS written in colourful chalk, with the words

GOOD OLD-FASHIONED
VANILLA ICE CREAM

peeking out from under the cloth.

"We need something for people who don't want too much adventure in their lives," said Mum, rubbing Limpet's hair.

"Mummm!" he complained, because he was ten years old and ten-year-olds didn't have their hair rubbed in front of their friends. But he was delighted. No silly ice cream. No crazy ice creams. No earwig and old trainers ice cream or whatever. Just vanilla ice cream. Like a normal shop.

"Before we open, I want to treat you kids," said Mum.

Limpet, Amelia and Norman sat at the little table outside the shop. Norman tied Curtis's lead to the table leg and threw some seeds on the ground for the scrawny but very happy chicken to peck at.

Limpet stretched out his legs and relaxed. He felt better about everything now. Not as worried. No fizziness inside him. No lemons causing luck to go haywire. No, he felt pretty good for the first time in a while.

And, even better, he was about to get some ice cream. Some great ice cream. Some great *vanilla* ice cream.

Limpet's sister burst out from the shop and squeezed into the chair beside Limpet.

"Move over!" he told her.

"*You* move over, Limpy," she said.

"I don't want to hear you slurping," said Limpet.

"I don't want to hear you *burping*," said Eve.

Norman and Amelia couldn't help themselves laughing.

Limpet's mum returned with four bowls on a tray. Limpet's face sank. In each bowl was spaghetti, with red sauce ladled all over it.

"Ooh," said Amelia.

"What is this?" said Norman.

Limpet's mum pulled the cloth from the board to reveal another one of TODAY'S SPECIALS:

SPAGHETTI
ICE CREAM

"Ta-dah," she said.

"Ta-doh no," groaned Limpet. No one would want spaghetti ice cream. It didn't even look like ice cream. It looked like spaghetti bolognese. Pasta. Tomato sauce. Piled neatly in a bowl.

No one wants spaghetti bolognese on a hot day. No one in the whole world.

"Oh, hold on!" said Mum. "I almost forgot something."

She dashed back into the shop and returned with a small bowl of white shavings, which she sprinkled over each dish. "Parmesan cheese," she said.

"*Mummm*," said Limpet. He knew he'd be saying "*Mummm*" a lot today.

"Try it," she said, smiling mischievously.

Limpet played with the food, but didn't want the shock of tasting meaty ice cream. Or tomatoey ice cream. Or pasta ice cream. Or cheese ice cream. Or whatever weirdness this was. He just knew it would taste—

"Amazing!" cried Norman so loudly it frightened Curtis.

"Oh wow, it really is *incredible*," said Amelia.

Eve was already nearly finished. She had demolished the spaghetti ice cream like it was the greatest thing she had ever tasted.

Limpet wondered if his friends were just being kind.

"Go on, Limpet," said Mum. "You might be surprised."

He pushed his spoon into the spaghetti, where the sauce met the pasta. It felt different. Like mushy spaghetti. He scooped up a small amount and brought it reluctantly to his lips. Everyone was watching him – including Curtis with her freaky chicken eyes.

He tasted the dish. "Impossible!" he said. It didn't taste *at all* like it looked. "It tastes of strawberry and the greatest vanilla ice cream I've ever had. And the white stuff is chocolate not cheese."

"See," said Mum. "It's good to try new things."

"It looks just like spaghetti," said Norman. "But it's *not* spaghetti. I'm so confused."

"The idea comes from Germany," said Limpet's mum. "They call it spaghetti-ice and they *all* eat it there. But nobody makes it here. Until now."

Limpet shovelled big spoonfuls into his mouth. He couldn't get enough of it. Eve had finished hers and tried to take some of his, but he used his spoon to knock hers away – like a sword fight. Only with little spoons.

"Have you ever made a Brussels sprout ice cream?" asked Norman. "Brussels sprouts taste like really lovely burps."

"Don't give her ideas," asked Limpet.

"I know a really good roundabout where we can get some very special Brussels sprouts," said Norman.

"Definitely don't give her those ideas!" begged Limpet.

But Mum already had loads of ideas. Crazy ideas. Impossible ideas.

And as Limpet scraped his bowl to get the last of the spaghetti ice cream, while his new friends sat very happily outside the Shop of Impossible Ice Creams, he began to think that maybe they weren't bad ideas at all.

"OK, it's time to open the shop," Mum announced with a clap of her hands. She put her finger to a light switch. "Actually, why don't you do it, Limpet?"

"Really?" asked Limpet.

"Yes," she said. "I've a feeling you'll bring the shop good luck."

Limpet felt a shiver run through his spine.

He'd had enough luck to last him a long, long time. Now, he just wanted everything to be A-OK.

Limpet turned the little sign on the door. OPEN.

They waited. And waited.

The promenade was quiet. A few seagulls looked for scraps. Curtis the scrawny chicken watched them with her freaky chicken eyes. Limpet, Norman and Amelia – their bellies full of spaghetti ice cream – stood nervously and hoped that someone, anyone, would come along.

Finally, in the distance they spotted that someone.

It wasn't just anyone. It was the hairiest man in Splottpool.

Chapter 34

Good news about the shop spread quickly through Splottpool.

They didn't need leaflets. They didn't need the bike. They just needed a hairy man on a skateboard to skate through the town, eating his ice cream while exclaiming how delicious it was, how unusual, how *impossible*.

"Ye have to try it!" he said. "Parsnips! PARSNIPS! And spaghetti. SPAGHETTI!"

People came to the shop to see what this strange fuss was all about. They stayed to . . . well, the only way to say it is that they stayed to stuff their faces with ice cream.

They read the menu and wondered if they should just stick with the GOOD

OLD-FASHIONED VANILLA ICE CREAM.

But it turned out they were adventurous sorts in Splottpool, so they tried the impossible ice creams.

The roast parsnip ice cream. The baked beans ice cream. The spaghetti ice cream. *Especially* the spaghetti ice cream.

They loved it. They asked for more. And then some more. And then a bit extra again.

The little shop soon had a queue out the door.

Limpet, Amelia and Norman helped take orders, serve ice creams, and clean up, while Mum took the money and Eve chased seagulls away from the front door.

"Roast parsnip ice cream!" someone said. "It's so different, and so sweet."

"I can't believe how good this baked beans ice cream is," someone else said.

"I need the toilet. Now!" screamed a small

boy, because that's what little kids always do.

From the counter, looking out through the little window, Limpet saw Mr Fluffy's van drive slowly up the promenade, stopping briefly.

There were no lights. No disco music. No ice creams. Just a very grumpy man looking out of the van window with a scowl.

Curtis escaped her lead and flapped straight at him. Mr Fluffy panicked, tried to roll up the window and drive away at the same time, only for his van to jolt and judder and sputter and stop before he finally got away just before Curtis got there.

Limpet laughed. And laughed. And laughed.

And then served up another helping of spaghetti ice cream to a woman.

"Good luck with your new shop," said the woman.

And Limpet laughed even more.

Acknowledgements

Like a great ice cream, a book needs the best ingredients and expert hands to make it special, so I'm hugely grateful to everyone who helped bring *The Shop of Impossible Ice Creams* to life.

Thank you to the whole team at Hachette – I definitely landed in a lot of good luck when I got to work with them. Thanks to stellar editor Rachel Wade and also to Hilary Murray Hill, Ruth Alltimes, Kate Agar, Nicola Goode, Lucy Clayton, Emily Finn, Samuel Perrett, Katie Maxwell, Ruth Girmatsion, Valentina Fazio, Eshara Wijetunge, Elaine Egan and Siobhan Tierney.

Huge thanks as always to my agent Marianne Gunn O'Connor, whose encouragement and enthusiasm is boundless.

A very special thanks to Selomé Reddy for being one of the very first readers of this story. *Danke* to Birgit Salzmann, Anke Müller and Gerd Krüger for introducing me to the wonders of 'spaghetti ice cream' on a trip to Marburg, Germany.

And finally, my love and thanks to Maeve, Oisín, Caoimhe, Aisling and Laoise. I owe you all an ice cream.

Are you ready for another helping of delicious adventure?

(What a question . . . of course you are!)

Read on for a sneak peek at the next book in

The Shop of IMPOSSIBLE ICE CREAMS

series

Chapter 1

Things were going pretty well in in Limpet's life.

He had written them down in his new notebook of Things That Have Gone (Really) Right.

In his new home of Splottpool, he had made new friends Amelia and Norman, and Norman's pet chicken Curtis.

His mum's Shop of Impossible Ice Creams was going very well, even with its strange ice creams like spaghetti ice cream and baked beans ice cream and roast parsnip ice cream.

The evil ice cream owner Mr Fluffy had NOT crushed their shop.

Yes, things were going pretty well for Limpet. But they would be going a lot better if he wasn't dressed as a giant cucumber.

"Why am I dressed as a giant cucumber?" he asked his mum, his face poking through the hole in the costume.

"Because it'll be a really fun way to let everyone know about our Shop of Impossible Ice Creams," she said as she carried her suitcase to her little car waiting outside their small shop on Splottpool's seaside promenade. "And also to let people know about our new, super-delicious cucumber ice cream."

"And why does the cucumber costume smell of onions?" Limpet asked, sniffing dramatically.

"Because I forgot my bag when I went to the shop so used the cucumber costume to carry onions," said Mum.

"And why isn't Eve dressed as a giant vegetable?" he asked, pointing at his very evil six-year-old sister sitting in the car with the window rolled down.

"Fruit," said Eve, chewing a gummy bear while sticking her tongue out at Limpet.

"What?" said Limpet, reaching in through the hole at the front of his cucumber costume to pick some onion skin from his mouth.

"Cucumbers are a fruit," said Eve.

Limpet did not know that cucumbers were a fruit. He did not know how Eve knew they were a fruit. But he did know Eve was pure evil for telling him.

"Eve's not in a costume because she's allergic to costumes," said Mum. "Remember that time she dressed as an Oompa-Loompa and actually went orange for a week afterwards?"

Limpet did remember the time Eve went orange for a week. She looked so silly and was terribly embarrassed.

That had been the best week of Limpet's life.

"Anyway, Eve's coming away with me for a week to see Granny," said Mum.

"And why can't I go to visit Granny instead of wearing an oniony cucumber costume?" asked Limpet.

"Because you have to help your father run the ice cream shop while I'm away," said Mum.

Limpet's dad popped his head out of the shop. He didn't live with Limpet and Eve any more, but had offered to stay for the week to spend some time with Limpet and mind the shop. And right now he was juggling onions.

"Don't worry about me," he said, still juggling, his tongue out as he concentrated. "I know what I'm doing."

Dad banged against a machine and ice cream sprayed down on his shoes. When he bent down to clean it, he banged his face off a tray of sparkly silver sprinkles.

Limpet sighed.

Limpet's mum sighed even louder.

"Dad can't make ice cream, but I've left enough in the shop to the last the whole week while we're away. Mushy peas ice cream. Fried onion ice cream. And, of course, cucumber ice cream. It means everything will be

A-OK until I get back."

"Fine, I get it," said Limpet, even though those flavours never sounded A-OK to him, no matter how many customers ate them up. "But I still don't want to wear this stupid cucumber costume."

Mum gave him a hug and kiss on the top of his cucumber head. "You're a great help, thanks. I couldn't run this shop without you."

Limpet squirmed, even though he secretly liked the kiss on his head, even if it was under the oniony cucumber costume.

Mum closed the car boot, got into the driver seat. Wriggling, she pulled a chocolate flake out from under her bottom.

"Yum," said Eve, grabbing the mushed chocolate flake from her and eating it.

Just as Mum was about to leave, they heard a whistle in the gentle breeze. It was the postwoman, cycling up the promenade towards them.

Dad came outside, wiping silver sprinkles from his eyebrows.

"Hey, you in the courgette costume," the passing postwoman called to Limpet as she cycled past. "I've some post for you."

Without stopping she handed a small, square envelope towards Limpet, who just about caught it with his foam green hands.

"Thanks," Limpet called after the cycling postwoman. "Oh, and I'm a cucumber!"

The envelope looked important.

The Shop of Impossible Ice Creams Splottpool

Dad took the envelope and pulled a card from it. Holding the card in his sparkle-covered hands, he read out loud:

"A JUDGE FROM THE GOLDEN SPRINKLES AWARD FOR BEST ICE CREAM WILL BE COMING TO YOUR SHOP . . ."

JOIN BOOT

ON A DANGEROUS ADVENTURE TO FIND WHERE
HOME IS, WHAT FRIENDS LOOK LIKE, AND
WHY HUMANS ARE SO LEAKY AND WEIRD.

SHANE HEGARTY
ILLUSTRATED BY BEN MANTLE

BOOT

SMALL ROBOT
BIG ADVENTURE

SHANE HEGARTY
ILLUSTRATED BY BEN MANTLE

BOOT
THE RUSTY
RESCUE

'FAST, FUNNY
AND FURIOUS'
EOIN COLFER

SHANE HEGARTY
ILLUSTRATED BY BEN MANTLE

BOOT
THE CREAKY
CREATURES

'FAST, FUNNY
AND FURIOUS.'
EOIN COLFER

Before becoming a full-time writer, Shane was a journalist and editor for the *Irish Times*, and worked in radio and the music business. He is the author of the bestselling series *Darkmouth* – which is currently being developed into a big-screen animation – and *BOOT*, which was his first illustrated series for younger readers.

He lives near Dublin with his wife and a brutally honest young readers focus group – otherwise known as his four children.

Photo Copyright © Ger Holland

For as long as Jeff can remember the only two things he's really wanted to do have been draw and tell stories. (Eating burritos fits in there somewhere too.) His passion for visual storytelling has led him to the fantastic world of children's illustration. Jeff's work has appeared in picture books, graphic novels, magazines, educational materials and on television.

He lives in Ohio with his amazing wife and their four equally amazing, talented, brilliant and inspirational kids. His favorite ice cream flavour is Red Skies at Night.

Photo Copyright © Elizabeth Crowther